BUILD
UNIVERSES

CW00550266

Rebecca Bettarini

Beauty Queen

© 2020 **Europe Books**
www.europebooks.co.uk

ISBN 979-12-201-0449-4
First edition: December 2020

Beauty Queen

This book is dedicated to Venezuela, a marvellous country where I had the luck to spend part of my childhood.

I wish to thank my parents Carla and Roberto for they gave me the opportunity to live a life full of adventures in extraordinary places. I wish to thank George for always being at my side in any new adventure. Gianfranco Bochicchio for his vigilant corrections
As well as all the people that will read this book.
Thank you

Any resemblance to real events and/or to real persons,
living or dead, is purely coincidental.

CHAPTER 1

Moscow

The spotlights lighten the platform. I look out from behind the curtain trying to focus on the empty seats. I close my eyes dazzled by the light beam pointed at me. I try to strain my eyes to see something beyond it. Nothing. Only a black room. Which will soon swallow me up.

"What are you doing here, Venezuela?" a voice behind me makes me rattle. I put my hand on my chest. He's only the lighting technician. If he had been the cameraman I would have tried to seduce him, after all it is the cameraman who takes the shots, and if he frames you in the wrong way your career is over. Even before it has started. But the lighting technician has no power.

"Nothing" I say adjusting my sash on my chest. The guy looks at me like if I am waisting his time "Come on Venezuela. Go get ready, it will be your turn soon."

I step quickly back into the dressing rooms. As soon as I walk in the other 99 finalists are getting ready. There are mirrors everywhere, dazzling spotlights on; costume designers making the finishing touches to stage clothes; crazy makeup artists and hairdressers who keep on smoothing, ironing, curling the hair of the Misses.

"Where are my extensions?" screams Guatemala. "I can't go out there without my extensions!!" like a fury, she walks around the space, poking between brushes, combs and sequins. Impetuously she screams out towards the Thai competitor. "Tell me the truth. You hid them from me!"

Thailand smiles from under miles of fake eyelashes. "Me?" She blinks innocently. "Why me!?".

"Because you hate me, that's why," Guatemala is furious. "You know that I'm more beautiful than you and you're trying to sabotage me. You did the same thing during the semifinals!"

"What are you babbling about!" answers Thailand.

"Don't say it's not true," Guatemala stricken back "at the semifinals you made my extensions disappear. Mexico found them in the trash bin! Isn't it Mexico?" she points in the direction of the Acapulco candidate.

"What's going on here!?" one of the organisers intervenes.

"Thailand hid my extensions, I can't go on stage without it!" she is on the brink of a hysteric crisis.

"Don't cry Guatemala! You can't either go on stage with drained makeup and puffy eyes" he puts a hand on her shoulder.

"Come on, now we'll get you some more extensions," he drags her away.

"Hey Venezuela, it's your turn" says a hairdresser brandishing a hair straightener. "We have no time to waste!" He grunts "Only 45 minutes left to the show".

"Sure," I say with mocking condescension and sit on the chair while looking at myself into the mirror. *God, I'm beautiful. I am a goddess.*

"So, what had we decided during rehearsals?" He asks to her assistant who flips through a book.

"Venezuela ... Venezuela ... Here it is! Bushy hairstyle and lots of cotton" says the girl. The hairdresser touches my hair.

"Your hair is too thin honey, it will never get that much volume" he thinks he knows, but he knows nothing.

"Honey" I reply with fake sweetness while my lips curve into a cynical smile. "Don't you worry. My hair will hold up just fine"

"But it's impossible," he says.

"Don't worry, do as I tell you," I insist firmly.

Twenty minutes later I have a cottoned big head and sublime brown curls that brush against my shoulders. "Wow!" he says "I never thought we would be able to give you all this volume!" he says incredulously. I look in the mirror satisfied with the result.

"There is a trick, my dear, but I won't tell you what it is!" I say getting up from my chair and walk towards the make-up artist.

"I want the same," Miss France whines. "How did you manage to make her hair so beautiful?"

"I don't know," he says embarrassed.

"You don't know? I want you to do the same thing to my hair, right now!" she squeaks. I gloat. My secret recipe for voluminous hair always leaves everyone amazed. The secret is to wash your hair with laundry soap, but no one has ever noticed it, because I always wait to be completely alone in the room before taking out the bottle of soap and spread it on my head. Even today I waited for Miss Kenya, with whom I share the room, to go out before getting in the shower. It is one of the many beauty secrets that I have been taught in the Dream House, and it is where it belongs to. You can't spread it around.

"So how do we makeup her?" asks the fat woman who stands before me, to her assistant. "Here it is," the skinny assistant says while glancing at a picture from the folder.

"A sophisticated makeup with the eyelid tinged out so as to lengthen the eye and gull-winged eyebrows" indicates parts of my face with the little finger. "Sculpted cheekbone and very clear base" he adds "I would use foundation number 02 to enhance the complexion and blush color 03 to give tone to the cheeks"

"Okay," says the fat woman, starting to rub the brush into the eyeshadow's powder.

I follow the operations step by step through the mirror. The line is fine, the blush is fine, the eyebrows … Wait a minute! I see myself in the mirror the eyebrows are not ok,

"You have to make my eyebrows look more curved" I say. The girl looks at me with despises.

"Darling, I have been doing this job for 30 years," she says controversially.

"And I have been preparing for this evening for the last 15 years" I say icy "so please make my eyebrows look more curved". The fat lady rolls her eyes and snorts.

If you want to fight I am ready. I look at her defiantly and, for an infinite second, we stare at each other.

"It's okay," she says, raising her hands and starting dipping the brush back into the dark brown mixture. "Are you happy now?" she adds with a note of sarcasm. I look at myself in the mirror "Yes, It's perfect."

"Next one!" the fat woman calls to the girls as my chair is immediately filled by Miss Argentina.

"30 minutes to go!" a voice from the speaker blasts. The tension rises. I have to take two more tablets! I go to my bag placed on the ground next to a chair. To get there I have to zigzag between dozens of costumes of feathers and sequins scattered around the room together with microscopic swimsuits, enervated hairdressers, agitated make-up artists and girls that are more hysterical than me. Tension could be cut with a knife. All of us competitors go from hysteria to euphoria. As always, before the final. I reach my bag and take out a small clutch from which I take Doctor Fliss' pills. They serve to regulate your mood. It is not really an antidepressant, but it prevents you from crying. As you can imagine an aspiring Miss cannot cry on the catwalk. She must smile and look happy at all times. This is what Dr. Fliss's pills are for. I swallow the pills down by bending my neck back.

"Oh here you are" says Antonio making his way among

the mass of half-naked girls who go around in circles like chickens in a chicken coop.

"Antonio, where were you!? You left me here alone!" I protest

"I was talking to Donald Trump! The organization says you are in the favourite shortlist !!"

I look at him happy. "Really?!"

But Venezuela is always in the list of favorites, after all our country has produced 7 queens in 62 years of competition, and holds the record of being the biggest Miss Universe producer. Not only. For 32 times the Venezuelan candidate has made it into the 10 finalists so it is not indicative to say that I, Cecilia am among the favourites, Venezuela is always ranking into the favourites.

"So let's reharse again," says Antonio "Do you remember how you have to walk?" he asks sitting in front of me with his elbows on his knees.

"One leg in front of the other counting one second for each stride" I say looking into his eye "and the weight of the body must be transferred entirely from one leg to the other" I keep saying "in order to sway."

"Sway obvious, but not cheeky!" says Antonio. "Perfect. And how do you have to hold your arms?" he asks "relaxed but my shoulders must be straight and stiff".

Antonio nods concentrated in front of me "And when you get to the bottom of the platform?" he asks "I stop and look at the audience and the jury straight in the eyes, I count down to five. Then I make a small turn and as I go back, I turn my head again with a smile and wink"

"Exactly!" Antonio says getting up "Bravo!"

"10 minutes to go," blasts the voice from the direction. "All the queens are asked to make their way to the stage."

My blood freezes in my veins. The tension is high. It's the same every time. Moments before going out on stage, a fire pervades your stomach, your salivation accelerates, your heart beats fast, the blood pulses in your temples and your legs tremble. This used to happen to me once, but now, thanks to Dr. Fliss' pills, my emotions are erased so unlike the other girls, when I go on the catwalk I am artificially relaxed and concentrated. I know exactly what I need to do. Where I have to go. How should I move. What should I say and with what intonation.

"Then I'm going to tell your mother that you're all right," says Antonio.

"See you in half an hour after the first elimination".

"Good luck. And may God bless you!" He adds.

"Seven minutes left!"

I quickly look at myself in the mirror tightening the heavy earrings to my lobes. I take a deep breath inhaling the scent of hairspray that fills the air. I close my eyes for a moment, squeezing in my hand the image of Santa Ávila on my necklace.

"Santa Ávila, make everything go well and protect me" I hiss under my breath before making the sign of the cross. I take off my dressing gown and remain in a swimsuit with the sash across my chest. I gather ideas for a moment and I'm ready.

"Minus 5,4,3,2,1 on Air!" The images of the ballet that we recorded the other day scroll across the screen as a jingle. In the theatre crowded with people, banners of support for the various Misses stand out. There is one for me too with the words "Cecilia Mendoza you and Los Roques are the pride of Venezuela".

We are lined up one next to another standing still on the red crosses glued for us on stage. The hands on the hips, the smile printed on the face and the big toe of the right foot pointed on the ground to bend the knee artfully. While the spotlight dazzles us, the presenter makes his microphone debut "Ladies and gentlemen. Welcome to the final of Miss Universe 2014!" Thunderous applause. We are here with the 100 finalists live from Moscow City Hall. Special thanks to the welcome that this beautiful city has reserved for us: *spasiba*! He yells into the microphone, sending the audience into raptures.

Here I am. After years of dreams and hopes I'm finally here. It doesn't seem true to me. It was all thanks to my mother. Dad abandoned my mother, me and my sister to our fate after finding another woman and having fled to Colombia. Mum had tried to report the disappearance of her spouse to try to cash a modest check from the Government, but everything had resolved into nothing. So mom had to roll up her sleeves and find a job that would allow her to feed us. She had worked in a bar in Paseo de la Castellana, but the owner, one evening under the effect of ron, had gone out into the garden and started shooting in the air. Mum had asked herself, 'What if he shoots me instead of shooting in the air next time?' Not that she wasn't used to violence. In a country like ours, violence is everywhere. You get used to street shootings, to people carrying guns, to see people die for 50 bucks. What is 50 bucks for an American? Nothing, but for a Venezuelan they can buy you many dreams. She wasn't afraid either of dying. After all, she was very religious and thought that God would welcome her with open arms in Heaven, but she feared that if she left us alone, the Government would put my sister and me in an orphanage where we would be at the mercy of anyone and there we would have known the ugliness of the world. For this reason, mum had quit that job and after various vicissitudes, she finally managed to find a golden opportunity in the home of a European family.

"Europeans are so different from us" she uses to tell in the evening when she came home. "They respect you, they are kind, they don't scream at you. They drink very little and above all, they never talk about money."

Acknowledging the unfortunate situation of our family, the Lancaster's invited us to move to their apartment in El Rosal. I remember that we took the bus. My sister and I held hands, while mom smiled happily. For us, who came from Coche, a poor *barrio* on the outskirts of Caracas, it seemed the beginning of a new life. A dream come true. But the dream did not last long. Two years later, the Lancasters returned to Europe and overnight, my mother found herself once again on the street. With President Oriondo and autarky, the country plunged more and more into chaos. Nobody was looking for a maid anymore, and mom found a job as a janitor in La Guaira. Every morning we traveled more than 40 kilometres on the bus 43 crammed like sardines. Mum had obtained the opportunity to take us to school with her, so that we could do what she hadn't been able to do: study. "One day you will have a bright future!" She repeated to us looking into each other's eyes as we returned home. A shabby apartment where radio and television were, for my sister Dayanara and me, the only leisure.

Like every year, that evening we were glued to the TV watching the Miss Venezuela final. I remember the sight of all those sequins, the girls who were so beautiful: unreachable.

Outside our window there was only misery and poverty in the hollow faces of the people. While before my eyes stood those images of women who were even crowned queens.

"Look Cecilia!" my mother said to me, "You too will one day be one of them." In that precise moment I had decided that this was what I wanted from life. One day, I too would become Miss Venezuela!

The red lights of the cameras light up on our bright smiles. The TV presenter dressed up in a tuxedo starts talking. "Good evening, ladies and gentlemen, welcome to the final of Miss Universe 2014 live from Moscow City Hall! I'm Ben Clavier and tonight I'm happy to introduce you to the 100 most beautiful girls in the world!" a buzz rises in the hall while we continue to hold our breath. I look for the familiar face of my mother in the crowd, but in vain. My eyes cannot perceive anything more than indistinct silhouettes in the dark. Sideways I take a look at the other competitors, they too smile and stand still like me in the typical Miss plastic pose.

"I'm Raffaella Riotta and I'm from Italy," the girl is saying in front of me. But she does it with terror, as if she was telling a lie. It is the emotion that plays bad jokes, but it won't happen to me. I am prepared. With an artificial walk I move like a panther on the platform. Now I'm the one who's got a camera pointed straight in my face. It's my turn. I squint my eyes in a bewitching look while, with all my breath in my lungs, I scream into the microphone "Cecilia Mendoza. Venezueeeeelaaaa!" My tone is triumphant and to give further emphasis to the phrase I raise a hand towards the sky. A shower of whistles of admiration rises from the gallery. I put my hands on my chest as a sign of thanks. I wait for my quartet to finish presentations as I walk towards the scenes with big smiles and winking eyes to the audience.

As soon as I'm off the stage, my smile turns off and my gaze stiffens. Antonio waits for me with a bottle of water in his hand. He follows everything from the monitor behind the scenes.

"You were fantastic," he says as I tear the bottle from his hands.

"Is this with electrolytes?" I say pointing to the bottle.

"Sure, darling," he gestures.

"Tell me. How did I do?" I say while I drink."

"You were fantastic, unbelievable! Have you seen the other competitors? What a flat tone and what little liveliness they had? It looked like they were listing the shopping list!" he says staring at me "But you! You seemed to be inciting the people to revolution!"

It's the first thing they teach you at the Dream House: to be impactful. Why should a person notice you, among 100 other girls who say their name in a microphone? The answer is simple: because you stand out. Because you will put your soul into it and a pinch of healthy malice. Because you will look straight down the tube as if you were an Oscar winning actress. Because your voice will be warm and modulated as the diction teacher taught you.

Slowly all the other girls join us behind the scenes. The dazzling lights of the makeup are momentarily turned off, which brings the dressing room back to a normal temperature. I absentmindedly look around and my eyes pierce the American competitor's figure. Look at her she is sure that she will win tonight, but she is absolutely wrong.

"Come on girls, it's time for the first elimination!" says a lady from the organisation waving. "Hurry up!"

A few minutes later the names follow one another on stage.

"The first candidate to move forward is number 7: Argentina!".

I knew it I think to myself while clapping my hands in a plastic pose.

"Number 94: Spain!" he screams out as Miss Spain with watery eyes walks towards the edge off the stage.

"Number 4: Russia! 87: Ukraine. 44: Mexico!".

As Ben Clavier says a number, I feel closer to when he will call out number 22: Venezuela. It would be impossible that I won't pass the turn. That would be something never seen in the history of the competition that Venezuela does not pass the first selection and I don't think this will happen today.

"And finally the last number gentlemen ..." Clavier says suspensfully. "There are 81 girls standing on the stairs and only one place near me" the tension rises, the audience starts to rumble. "The last name is ...." masterful pause "With number 22 MISS VENEZUELA!" a scream of joy rises from the stands while, with simulated amazement, I am about to reach my colleagues.

Back in the dressing rooms the girls flounder. They are not professionals. They don't have a clue about how the pageant works. They just don't know anything. They are not prepared to face this day. They are thrown here haphazardly. They do not know that the advertisement will last five minutes and that the Miss from the previous edition will be interviewed. They do not know that it is useless to rush if we won't be getting out on stage before 10 minutes.

"I knew it, I knew you would make it!" Antonio ecstatically runs towards me. "Now concentrate! Tell me what the next step is."

I repeat what I will have to do like a brilliant student.

"Exactly, that's perfect! Let me get the costume for you." He disappears behind a fire door. I remain for a moment staring with detachment at the whirl in front of me. Crazy girls running up and down, hairdressers who work at full speed, make-up artists who touch up the smudges, mothers who try to enter the backstage and get pushed back by the security service. I am so happy that I am not an amateur anymore. How many pageants have I took part in my life? 28, 29? If we count the one in high school, I would say 29. All those pageants one after the other, to learn how to get here. A path made up of restless nights spent sewing costumes, hard regimes, a thousand auditions. All the money my mother had earned had been spent trying to get me into the Dream House. That place where they taught you to be a Miss with military discipline and a long series of aesthetic surgery interventions. Each year the school only admitted fifteen girls, but only the best student amongst them, would have been sent to pageants.

Antonio returns with my costume in his hands. Antonio has been working at the Dream House for years and is one of the few people I know I can trust. During my years in pageants, I learned several things. The first is that no one can be trusted, you can only rely on your agent. And Antonio has been my agent since I was the only one to be selected amongst the 15 girls.

And yet still now, from the top of my career any small mistake would have fatal consequences. For example, there was a Miss Venezuela who, years ago, had asked for a little extra surgery before the Miss Universe pageant. She ended up with a hopelessly devastated butt and not only had she not been able to take part in the Miss Universe competition, but the Miss Venezuela sash had also been revoked, in favour of the first runner-up. Due to such a small mistake, years of sacrifice had suddenly vanished. What could she have done next? Nothing, her career was over and what is worse is that she hadn't even had time to marry a millionaire before her life was destroyed forever.

As for me I hadn't become the best just for my slender figure. I am the best because of my immeasurable determination in achieving a goal. That goal that I had set myself to achieve at any cost.

A few minutes later, the splendid red evening gown wraps my artificially perfect body. Antonio makes me repeat the moves that I will have to perform out there. There are now five of us left and it all depends on me.

The girls who have been eliminated cry. "Why did they eliminate me, what's wrong with me?" They are sobbing in tears. God! How pathetic they are.

"What happened to my dress!" The Panama's competitor screams at the top of her lungs bringing me back to reality. She is holding in her hands the red evening gown she was to wear in a matter of minutes. The dress is irreparably torn apart and damaged from side to side.

"Who did this!!!?" She sobs by showing to everyone her wonderful dress that has now turned into a hideous rag. I can't help but snort with raised eyebrows. Amateur! Why do you think Antonio is storing my scene costumes away from here?

Now I'm the only competitor whose gown is red. I am not a bad person, but you understand I couldn't allow the Panamanian candidate to wear a gown the same colour as mine. The idea of cutting the dress crosswise to make it look like an accident was also brilliant. After all, the make-up carts are made of iron, and they could easily thad torn the chiffon of which the dress was made while hanging on a rack.

Finally, the announcer calls my name and I make my last entry into my floating dress, spreading my arms out as an angel. I have a big smile on my face, and a look that is the perfect synthesis of security, charm, malice and simplicity.

The choreography is now blue, which is why I chose a red dress. I knew from the rehearsals that the ending would have a choreography in shades of blue and that red would stand out. Large beams of light illuminate us from above while the indistinct buzz of the public grows together with our tension.

When answering the questions drawn in the ballot box, several Misses give really embarrassing answers. Not like me who have been preparing for years. I listen with slight apprehension to the question that the judges ask me. *I know it!*

I provide an answer calmly and with determination. The expression on the faces of the jury is satisfied.

A few minutes later the host announces the final moment. "In a few minutes we will crown the next Miss Universe!"

He slowly opens the envelope.

"Fourth runner-up. Miss Australia! " The Miss starts to cry.

"Third runner-up. Miss Panama!" The room bursts into a roar. Now it's just me and Miss Russia who are holding hands one in front of each other.

Santa Ávila don't abandon me now!

Countless seconds go by until Ben Clavier says "Miss Universe 2014 is ..." drum roll "The number 22! Cecilia Mendoza! Miss Venezuela!"

The room explodes between screams and thousands of cotillion drop from the ceiling. Miss Russia drowns me in a hug. My eyes get clouded.

The previous years' Miss crowns me and helps me wear the new sash around my chest.

"It will only last one year, put it to good use" she whispers.

A round of applause rises as I cross my hands thankfully while I take my first walk as a new crowned Miss universe. In that precise moment it all made sense. The sacrifices, the expectations, the hopes. I had won. I had succeeded. I had reached the top.

CHAPTER 2

New York

The black limousine pulled up in front of Fifth Avenue 56. The driver got out quickly to open the door for the new Miss Universe. Cecilia and Antonio quickly stepped into *the Splendid* condominium.

"Good evening, Miss," the doorman held the heavy crystal door for them.

"Good evening," she smiled back, looking at him from the height of 1,80 meters.

They both disappeared into the elevator. Antonio, who was next to her pressed the PH on the button panel.

"When will Miss America leave?" Cecilia asked him while looking at herself in the mirror.

"Next week," replied Antonio.

"Finally!" She snorted.

"You can't stand her anymore, can you?" Antonio could not hide the amusement that the spitefulness of the first women aroused.

"In fact, I really can't stand her. She is pretentious and on the top she distracts me. As you can imagine I have to keep on focus. I only have eleven months left as a Miss Universe and I have to take advantage of every minute of that time to build myself a career" she complained.

"You are right dear. In eleven months we won't work together any longer," he echoed.

Cecilia was aware that it was not easy to carve yourself a

way into that world. She was already 23, it was too late for her to start a professional modelling career. Even assuming that hypothetically she could get it, she wouldn't have had time to become a famous top model with a six figure pay-check. Moreover, nowadays fashion designer were only casting androgynous girls and she, a busty brunette couldn't stand a chance. She could have tried approaching Hollywood but it wasn't easy. Maybe she would have been cast as a hot chick in some movie. That could have been a start, but she knew that would be it. As she knew she couldn't act for toffees. The alternative was the classic one: find a sugar daddy and marry him. A cliché that, in a city like New York that was literally crawling with rich man, seemed easy to pursue, although there was hard competition. The only card in her pocket which would make her stand out, was her Miss Universe title. And that was gold.

Back in the elevator, they stopped on the 55th floor. Cecilia, who was still immersed in her thoughts, find herself back with her feet on the ground. Antonio pulled out the keys and opened the apartment door. A splendid penthouse with marble floors, large windows, a lounge always adorned with fresh flowers and a spacious kitchen.

"It seems like yesterday that we arrived in New York" exclaimed Antonio "When we first entered this apartment, I would have expected you to cry; just like all the other Miss before you did. But you, you surprised me by asking only where the gym was"

Cecilia shrugged "It seemed a relevant detail, since I have to train for three hours in a row seven days a week." She took off her fur coat and sat down on the comfortable white sofa in the living room. Antonio went to the kitchen where he served himself a glass of water. "Do you want something witch?" He glanced inside the fridge full of low-calorie products.

"No thanks!" she answered from the sofa.

"Miss America isn't home?" he asked closing the refrigerator.

"No. Today she had an interview for a fashion magazine," she explained listlessly.

"Really!?" he returned to the hall phlegmatically. Cecilia looked at his black hair that looked even darker when, like today, he wore a white shirt. "So, tell me, what is the program?"

"I didn't get the question"

"I mean, what am I supposed to do now? You know, after winning the Miss Universe pageant, what happens?"

Antonio smiled "what exactly do you expect to happen, witch?" He admired the ambition of this woman. She was always one step ahead.

"I do not know! What did the others do before me?" she asked him

"Well. They took advantage of the contracts that come with the title. You know. Fashion shows, advertising campaigns. The usual stuffs!"exclaimed cutting it short.

"And then what?"

"And then ... nothing! I'm sorry. What did you pictured exactly? A very few of them have made the stellar career you are thinking of right now." He tried to explain to her that it was not for granted. But the stubborn Cecilia pursued her ideas. "I want to know what happens when this is over?"

"And how am I supposed to know?!" Antonio admitted.

"I warn you. I will not get back to where I came from which is nothing. So you better start looking for projects for my future, and I am god damn serious about it." Her eyes darted.

"Ok, what kind of projects?" Antonio had been caught off guard.

"Whatever. I don't care! Go find something. I don't

know! It could be a contract with a top designer, or a role on some television program in Latin America! Or you can find me an agent in Hollywood! Whatever!". Antonio remained thoughtful. He certainly could have her signing some contracts in the world of fashion, but he was sure that couldn't last long. He opened up in total honesty "Look. I don't really think many brands will be interested in cooperating with you when you no longer have a crown on your head."

She snorted "Okay look! I don't want to waste my time! So find me something, anything! Then I'll figure it out on my own, as usual." She stood up from the sofa and went to her room to get changed.

CHAPTER 3

Washington

Sitting in his office the Director of the CIA Carter, had high hopes to receive good news from his secret informants. The operation they were working hands on day and night, had already taken from him much more hours of sleep than the previous operations.

"Would you like a coffee, sir?" His assistant materialised in front of his table without him even noticing.

"Yes, thanks. As always an espresso-"

"-without sugar!" she eagerly added before he could complete his sentence. Olivia could have tell that her boss had been more worried than usual in the last few days. Maybe he had some problems at home. The idea that something could go wrong in the world's first espionage agency did not even crossed her mind. The phone rang just as Carter was enjoying his hot coffee.

"Any news?" he asked while holding his breath.

"I'm sorry. We failed yet another time." Instinctively Carter wanted to throw his phone down the window. *Shit! How is this possible?*

"You will receive a full report on the topic later today, sir." said the voice on the other side of the phone sweating cold. Carter ended the conversation impetuously. It was the third time that the fucking Orinoco operation failed. And soon his reputation would be flushed down the toilet.

CHAPTER 4

Los Angeles

The famous movie Director thought that in his entire life, he had never seen anyone act so poorly. "She is impossible to cast!" he scoffed to his assistant who looked back at him concerned. "What? Why are you looking at me that way? What did I say?" The assistant cleared his throat. "The problem is that she is a *friend* of the producer. She comes highly recommended!" he added with a grimace.

"And now what? How on earth am I supposed to cast a *Latina* in the role of a Swedish? For Christ sakes!?" The Director protested, waving the script he holds in his hand.

"Maybe we could change the script and say she is from South America?" The Director glared at him. "Just saying… It's just an idea" he justified himself.

"Fuck the producers and their *girlfriends*!" He rant cupping his head in his hand "Okay! Let's do this! What am I supposed to do here? This film will have to be finished sooner or later! Tell the agent that she is fine, come on hurry up!" He snorted as the assistant started to walk. "And tell the makeup artist to do his best to make her look Swedish, what the fuck! It's out of the question that we rewrite the whole script to cast this cocksucker"

"How did I go?" Cecilia jumped off the set in excitement. She wore a pink silk dress, which left very little to the imagination.

"You were amazing! Simply perfect in the snows of

Stockholm!" The Director forced himself to be convincing while standing up from his chair.

"Really?" Cecilia found it hard to believe "Then I have to tell *daddy* immediately," she said.

"Of course, honey! Call *daddy* and pass it on to me please". The girl quickly dialed the number on her cell phone and *daddy* answered immediately.

"Helloooo! Guess what? The Director said I'm fantastic for this role!" She meowed as the Director rolled his eyes. On the other end of the line, *daddy* had no doubts.

"Are you happy darling?" he said looking forward to what she would do to him that night in return. "Very, very much!" she chirped "Thanks, *daddy*!" She was genuinely excited about her first role in a Hollywood movie. The Director then made her a sign for her to hand the phone over to him.

"Dear producer! How are you? What a beautiful woman! A fantastic actress! The new Sofia Loren!"

"Yes, of course!" the producer said knowing the Director was genuinely toadying him.

"What about the rest? Is the movie making its way? Are we on schedule? Don't go over budget!"

"Don't worry. Everything is going great so far. We are perfectly in time!" The Director reassured him.

"Fantastic then! Keep it up!" the producer cut short, ending the conversation.

"So Ms. Mendoza. Talk to my assistant about the contract signing; he will tell you what time and what days you are expected on set."

Let's hope she won't get ahead of herself and starting playing diva, he thought to himself as he walked away.

CHAPTER 5

New York

Cecilia was sitting on the sofa she had bought at a final clearance in a discount store. Her year as a Miss went by too quickly. Wrapped up between photo shootings, interviews, and trips to some poor country for charity, she hadn't seen the time go by. Now she was no longer a Miss, just one of a thousand beautiful girls in search of fortune in the most competitive city in the world. The Hollywood producer who she had visited in Los Angeles frequently, when she still had her crown on her head, had cast her for some marginal roles in the other two movies he was producing. Although she has always been very *nice* to him, after a while he'd lost interest in her. He had replaced her with a younger and probably more interesting special friend.

"This is Hollywood, baby!" her agent told Cecilia the day he'd dumped her, saying he had no more time to waste with her. "At the beginning you are the hot novelty that rises interest; after six months, however, someone better comes along, and you end up in oblivion." He explained.

Antonio hadn't found much for her to do in New York either as her measurements were not standard for modelling. At that time beauty codes had changed, resulting in her provocative curves did not peak the interest of anyone.

Alone and sad, Cecilia had found an apartment not far from Central Park. It costed her an arm and a leg. The amount of money she had saved during her previous year's contracts, was getting thinner. Yes, she still had a few contracts as a brand image and also earned some cash with the interviews, but nothing that made her feel satisfied about her accomplishments. All these sacrifices, and years spent studying didn't lead her anywhere near to her dreams. She felt very angry.

The intercom rang. It was Antonio "little witch, it's me!" Cecilia walked towards the door listlessly waiting for her agent to enter. Tonight it was the last engagement she would attend as Miss Universe and which meant it was also the last time Antonio would accompany her to one of those lavishing jet set events. By looking at her expression, Antonio immediately sensed something was wrong with her. So, he asked for a clarification. "What's the matter with you Ceci? Are you sad?"

"I'm really tired," she curled up on the sofa, girding her knees, "I came up here thinking that I would conquer the world. And instead, I have done nothing!"

"Do not say that! You have conquered the crown of Miss Universe. Do you realize how far you've gone!?" He sat down next to her and put his hands around her shoulders.

"Look at me! I haven't done anything with my life! I'm not a model. I'm not an actress. I'm no longer a Miss anymore; and by the way I'm old! I'm 25, what the hell!"

"But you make good money with television interviews, don't you?"

"I do! But God knows how long those interviews will last! How long do you think people will still be interested in me, since new beauty queens are elected every year?"

This was the downside that Antonio was very aware of. It was the same path all the Misses went through. At first everyone was looking for them; after a while they were crushed by the newly arrived.

"Let's do this," he said, looking straight into her eyes.

"Get ready for tonight's gala event, and we'll find you a husband. A good one with deep pockets so that you can secure your life at least financially and stop live alone you in this horrible apartment, whining all day. What do you say?" Cecilia breather heavily embracing her resignation, that was the only thing left to do.

Two hours later, the car approached the famous MET stairs. A charity ball was held that evening organized by one of the most prestigious associations in New York. Despite the spring temperatures, Antonio was wearing a velvet tuxedo as he dropped to Cecilia the impressive guest list of the evening.

"There will be VIPs and people from Wall Street. So don't worry, they're filled with cash!"

Cecilia was squeezed into a spectacular red haute couture fashion dress. She was convinced that if red had brought her luck once, it would have brought her luck again. The spectacular lighting of the facade of the Metropolitan Museum of Art anticipated the elegant and sophisticated atmosphere that guests would find inside. Antonio and Cecilia climbed the steps together. Antonio cavalierly escorted Cecilia under his arm. Photographers directed their lenses towards all the guests, and shouted out loud the names of the most prestigious ones in order to make them strike a pose under a bombardment of flashes. A journalist crossed the barriers winding a microphone in her hand "I am from Latin America TV, can I interview you?" She went straight to Cecilia

"Sure!" Cecilia said immediately. The red camera light started flashing.

"How does it feel to be the most beautiful woman in the world?" The journalist shouted to be heard in that confusion

"It's a big responsibility," replied Cecilia, looking straight down the tube. "But you know. I am no different than other women, some days I see myself beautiful and other days I feel really ugly. This applies to everyone."

The journalist smiled, and Cecilia went on "... you have to identify yourself with normal women and make people know that if I don't have cellulite it's only because I fight it every day!"

The reporter nodded. "You are wearing a fantastic dress! Can I ask you who designed it?"

"Oscar della Renta" she said with a shrug.

"Very beautiful! How does Miss Universe 2014 spend her days?" he asked curiously.

"I wake up early. I do a 3 hours training, then I read international newspapers and I dedicate myself to the charitable activities of which I am the spokesman. Like the melting of glaciers in the North Pole and sick children. Then I work as a model and I am a testimonial of various brands, I take classes of diction and acting and in the evening, when I get home, I talk to my family members who I miss a lot. In fact, I would like to take the opportunity to blow them a kiss!"

"What a good girl Miss Universe is! A serious and sweet girl who cares about family values! Many thanks for the interview." She turned away and left.

"Very good, little witch!" Antonio got excited.

They entered the museum, where magnificent flowers adorned the impressive rooms, crowded with people. Everyone wore splendid dresses. The jewels wore by the ladies were as big as fruits. Cecilia had never seen something like that, *it's wonderful!* She thought as she looked at the imposing building.

"Are you ready?" Antonio asked.

"I was born ready, honey!" She winked at him. "When you come from nowhere like I do, you don't just wait for life to serve you the opportunities on a silver tray. You go and get it for yourself. Whatever it takes," she added and walked into the crowd.

Antonio stood still for a moment. Cecilia's fighting temper was back.

All of New York was there that night. Cecilia recognized actors, bankers, politicians and models. She decided that, to get noticed in such situation, she must not only be beautiful, but also cunning. "Antonio!" she rebuked him, peeking at him inserting some food into his mouth.

"I go to the bathroom. I'll be right back" she said, but she didn't. She didn't really go to the bathroom. She went patrolling the dinner hall to find out where was she sitting. In the impressive hall, the round tables were topped with spectacular decorations. Once at her table she found out that she would have been sitting next to two gentlemen who according to Google, were already married. She then decided to cross Internet information with the names of the other guests and thanks to this clever stratagem, when dinner began, she was sitting next to the most interesting eligible bachelors.

One was a Wall Street divorced tycoon. The other was a boy from Silicon Valley who had amassed an immense amount of money by developing an online dating app. She mischievously flirted throughout the dinner with both. She knew they would compete like two fighting cocks over a woman. Especially a woman as attractive as she was. And Cecilia encouraged them even more by playing the role of the mysterious woman, to perfection. At the end of the dinner, both men were at her feet. In the following weeks her phone was off the hook. They both called non-stop to invite her to dinner. She left them wait until, unexpectedly, she agreed to date them both on alternate nights for 2 months. She allowed them to give her incredible gifts, although pretending that it was not right to accept them. Men knew how to be very ingenious when they were interested and especially when they were extremely rich. Cecilia took the situation with disenchantment and pragmatism. She slept tight at night knowing that, if the story wouldn't work with one, there was a replacement ready.

The summer weeks went on beautifully as she was indulging into the attentions of the two men. Although she preferred the boy from the Silicon Valley she wasn't jumping at the idea of moving to San Francisco. In addition, the boy was young, which gave her little confidence. While the Wall Street banker.... She surely saw herself much more doing intense shopping sessions in the exquisite boutiques on the Fifth Avenue than at the Apple Store in Palo Alto. After a couple of months Tom, the lord of Wall Street, asked her to go and live together in his beautiful apartment on Park Avenue. Cecilia did not let him ask her twice, and three days later she rang at his doorbell. Tom was a sporty and charming 55-year-old gentleman. He didn't seem to be nearly thirty years older than her. He was divorced from his first wife and had three children; which made it unlikely that he wanted more. Cecilia didn't want any. *After what this body cost me, I don't really think about ruining it to give birth to a whining baby.*

In addition, the idea of abandoning her career opportunities and dedicate herself to a child did not appeal to her at all. So she dropped the Palo Alto plan even though she continued to see the boy without Tom's knowledge. Some kind of plan B if Tom hadn't asked her to marry him. But just like that and out of the blue, after a few months, Tom proposed and put a beautiful three-carat brilliant under her nose on a winter's morning in front of the bull on Wall Street. The most romantic place a Wall Street guy could think of.

Finally!

Cecilia could begin to relax. Now, even if she'd never became a movie star, or a famous model, she could easily survive in style for the rest of her life. Tom was, in fact, a good investment.

The wedding day was extraordinary. They tied the knot at the Plaza hotel, decorated with the most spectacular flowers imaginable. Antonio had called the *Cirque de la Lune* who performed extraordinary acrobatic shows around the ice statues. Tom had agreed to give each guest a branded handbag and many important people had attended the event. Cecilia's mother was moved. Eventually all those sacrifices had been not gone to waste as her daughter had come a long way. She recited a prayer to the Virgin of Ávila to thank her for how generous she had been with them. They were all very happy that day.

CHAPTER 6

Montecarlo

Like every year, Cecilia Mendoza was extremely bored in taking part at the Principality's vintage car rally. She didn't even know where this boredom came from. Everything she dreamed of as a child had come true. Of course, she had worked hard to get there, and her good star had also helped her. However, no matter how hard she tried, she was unable to be satisfied with her life.

Sitting in the *café de Paris* that morning, she sipped a passion fruit extract. She looked at everyone and everything with disinterest. Her husband was quite handsome and above all, rich. He had a Ferrari, a boat, and a house in all the cities where it was *cool* to have one. In addition to three beautiful children that her husband had with his ex-wife. What more can you ask life for?

It must be the boredom of those who already have everything ... she mumbled to herself ... what if I got a dog? She immediately rejected that silly idea. In fact, what really bothered her was that she hadn't managed to become famous. After the wedding she'd continued to wait and hope to work in movies. Among other things, she had managed to get cast in a small role in a Mexican soap opera, albeit without great results. Her husband had opened some doors for her to the golden world of Hollywood. Once again, although she had been generous to various producers, the Directors had deemed her face expressionless. In short, they had discarded her.

"In this life Cecilia you can't have everything" her mother repeated to her. But what did she knew! For Cecilia Mendoza the world had no limits. She was born to take it all!

Her husband brought her back to reality by blowing her a kiss on her forehead.

"Hello my love". He had to admit his wife was more beautiful every year. Not that he was surprised, given the bills he payed for her little interventions.

If only she didn't seem so bored and lifeless he thought.

She had become apathetic. When he had first met her and fell in love with her, she was not only beautiful - after all, New York was full of beautiful women - she was alive. This was what made her special, together with that kind of flame that burned inside of her and that led her to want more and more. Her ambition was enormous, and he mirrored himself into it. Of course, the fact that she had been a Miss was a plus. If all his friends were only dating models, there was only one Miss Universe winner per year, and it was his. His reputation had exploded since he dated her and their wedding was even mentioned in the New York Times, which led to him earn a lot of money that year. He had to admit that she had played smart making him wait longer than necessary and by throwing him into a competition with another younger and richer guy. In short playing the cat and mouse game. Something that, for someone like him, was irresistible. Although now...

"What are you doing dear?" Tom asked sitting down at the table.

"Nothing. I drink my extract," she answered listlessly.

"Have you been to the hairdresser?" He dared to ask as he could never tell the difference between the before and after those long hair-styling sessions his wife underwent.

"Yes"

"By the tone you say that you don't seem really satisfied"

"As usual" she continued while sip the yellow liquid in her glass and rolled her eyes around her. Always the same people. Always the same breakfast. Nothing ever changed. Nothing. It was always the same thing every day. Even the waiters who have been working in that café for more than thirty years never changed.

CHAPTER 7

Hotel de Paris

Agent Willis inspected the room. It was large and pompous like all the rooms in the *Hotel de Paris*. It was not easy to find a vacancy at that time of the year. The Director have had no hesitation when Willis' colleague introduced himself in incognito saying that a Silicon Valley billionaire would pay any amount for a room that night.

"It must be room 266. My friend wants only 266 and no other room" he had specified while the Director explained to him that there were even more spacious and prestigious suites available that featured even a private swimming pool on their terrace.

"He wants 266, take it or leave it." Given the resolution of his client, the Director hadn't thought too much about it. He was used to strange requests. *Rich people were like that. The more they have money, the more they have special requests.* He had wondered though why the 266. It was a room like any other, nothing more, nothing less. He thought it must had some kind of sentimental value for this gentleman. Maybe he had already stayed in that room before for a weekend with his ex-girlfriend, or something.

"*Bien sûr monsieur*" he put his bright teeth on display "*de suite*".

A few moments later, the garçon had showed him to his room. As soon as the garçon opened the door, and explained how the air conditioning worked and where the minibar was located, the agent gave him a generous tip to get rid of him as fast as possible. Once alone Willis shut the door closed and stared around with astonishment.

People have a lot of money, he thought, looking at the impeccably furnished spacious and elegant beige lounge. He looked at the clock. In a few moments his colleagues would have knocked on the door. He approached the window, moving the heavy blue curtains that prevented him from glancing out. The targets were sitting at the bar, quietly. He decided it was safe enough to open the window to check upon the situation. A warm summer breeze caressed his face. The morning sun shone high in the blue sky.

Now I understand why rich people love this place, he thought, breathing in the pleasant and clean air of Monaco. He peered down. There were still people coming out from the casino. Incredible cars were parked in the square around the fountain. All the ladies wore elegant clothes, while the men wore watches that probably cost more than what he earned in five years.

So it is life he told himself. He took a deep breath and turned his gaze once more to his watch. *Two minutes to go.*

Meanwhile, at the tables of the café de Paris, located right in front of the hotel, Cecilia browsed into a fashion magazine, while Tom, sitting by her side, thought it had probably been a mistake to marry a girl like that. Although it was cool at first to have a beautiful woman like his wife next to him, now, after being married for three years, he couldn't stand her anymore. Her attitude started to bother him as he was pissed about having her around the house, especially when she complained all day because she couldn't break through in movies. She was way different than when he'd met her as she was no longer the *hot latina* who had achieved the impossible. Now, to Tom's eyes, she wasn't any longer of interest. She was no longer a number one, she was a looser who was slowly letting herself go into frustrations. The flame of ambition Cecilia had before, had burned out almost completely, leaving way to her comfortable and routinely life made of shopping and other very superficial interests she had. Tom was deadly bored with her. He found her uninteresting and was seriously determined to leave her. Cecilia on her side, had more or less noticed that something was wrong in their relationship. But she thought it was better to pretend not to notice. If she'd caught him with his hands in the marmalade, she would have ripped him off way more money than the sum negotiated in their prenuptial agreement. This is what her New York attorney had explained to her. Indeed, in the past few months, Tom had started a relationship with a girl much younger than him. A very well-known and sexy influencer. One of those girls who had managed to get exactly where they wanted in life, and this fact seriously turned Tom on. When he was with her, he felt strong, young, full of energy and cheerfulness. Instead, at home with Cecilia, he felt suffocated. His wife had lost the *joie de vivre.*

"Tonight we are invited to the Villa Les Fleurs' party" he hoped that at least this news would put her in a good mood. After all, at least at the beginning, Cecilia loved attending the principality's sparkling parties.

"Is it full length attire?" She glanced at him from the edge of her glass.

"Obviously," he frowned.

"Well, then I'll have to call the maid to tell her to prepare my green gown," she pulled the cell phone out of her microscopic handbag.

"As you wish, honey" Tom continued to sip his cappuccino.

At 10:30 the bell in room 266 rang as expected. Agent Fox and agents Brown and Smith entered the room discreetly.

"How's the situation?" Fox asked Willis.

"Normal."

"Do we have a good view over the targets?" Smith asked.

"Affirmative, Sir! The targets are right in front" he pointed his finger at the window.

"Well. The team will proceed in a few minutes. Brown! Inspect the movements on the street"

"Yes sir" he said proceeding towards the window.

"Are we sure they don't suspect anything?" Smith asked Willis.

"Negative, sir. They don't suspect anything."

"Very good Willis! Excellent job!" he complimented him.

"Sir. The car is approaching," said Brown.

"Agent Fox! Go down, now!" Smith instructed.

"Yes, sir!"

Carefully, agent Fox opened the door of room 266 and began to walk on the large green carpet that lined the corridor. He wore a white suit, which made him look very elegant. Earlier that day he had showed up at the hotel with a vintage car, a gold watch and a beautiful blonde, just to go unnoticed among all those rich people. When he entered the hall all the ladies had turned their heads intrigued by this so well dressed and handsome boy. A perfect coverage.

"*Bonjour monsieur*" the concierge opened the door for him. Fox smiled and put his sunglasses on his nose. Now his eyes looked directly at the targets: Tom Forrester and Cecilia Mendoza, who, unaware of everything, were having breakfast. Smith looked towards the black van in which his companions were ready to launch the operation.

"Agent Fox give the signal whenever you want," Smith's metallic voice croaked in the headset.

"Ok," he said, pretending to look at his watch to distract the attention. With large steps and a newspaper under his arm, he approached the café passing right in front of the casino entrance. He asked the waiter who was carrying a delicious omelette in his hand, to find him a free table. His eyes met the gaze of Cecilia Mendoza who stared at him intensely for a moment.

"The target looked at me," Fox whispered into the headset.

"Shit!" swore Smith "maybe they know! Keep them busy, Fox" Smith instructed. Fox then walked over to the Forrester's table with his best smile on display.

"Excuse me if I ask you, ma'am, but aren't you by any chance Miss World?" it was the signal that his companions were waiting for.

"Here we go! Here we go! Hurry up!" Smith shouted to the whole team in the headset.

Cecilia showed a huge smile to this beautiful boy "Yes. Actually it's me!" she prayed "But in reality you know, I was Miss Universe and not Miss World. You know, they are two different pageants …" Her husband rolled his eyes and immersed himself even more into the newspaper reading. In just a snap four agents pulled out their badges in front of their table.

"Mr. Forrester?" said Agent Tercer.

"Yes, it's me," he replied unsuspecting.

"Interpol. You're under arrest for insider trading." The agent handcuffed him like in the movies. Cecilia instinctively squeezed the arm of Agent Fox who in return, grabbed her with both hands and dragged her towards the van.

Tom started screaming "it's a mistake! I'm innocent! I'm not the guy you're looking for!" He shouted "Cecilia! I swear! I have done nothing!"

"Shut up! Anything you say can be used against you, so shut up!" Tercer explained, dragging him forcefully towards the van. Cecilia was paralyzed by fear "Tom? What have you done, Tom!?" She searched for an explanation in her husband's brown eyes, before then in his words.

"I didn't do anything darling! They are wrong!"

An agent pushed Tom into the van.

"I can not believe it!" Cecilia began to cry "son of a bitch! Fuck you!"

"No Cecilia! I am innocent, I swear to you!" Tom shouted in front of the astonished eyes of the whole crowd in the square that remained silent for a second, before returning to its usual routine.

"That's what everyone says, Mrs. We never arrest guilty people. You will have to come with us to be interrogated," Fox added.

"Me? I do not know anything!" she glared at him.

"Unfortunately, it's routine, ma'am," he explained.

"Come on Barbie, no more questioning. Get in the car!" Roared Tercer as Cecilia tried to resist. "If you don't come on your own I'll be forced to handcuff you" Angry, Cecilia slipped her long legs into the car. "You don't need to handcuff me, you imbecile."

Once in the car she took a deep breath trying to push back the tears that were pulsing in the edge of her eyes to get out.

"What the fuck! In front of all of Montecarlo!" she bursted.

Smith seated next to Tercer who was driving, glanced at Cecilia from the rearview mirror. He knew she was beautiful, but he couldn't imagine she was so much beautiful.

"Don't worry, madame," he said without taking his eyes off her nipples clearly sticking out from under the white blouse. "60% of people that live in Monte Carlo have problems with justice" he confessed.

"And why are you taking my husband away, then? What did he do? We are honest people, where are you taking him?" she was on the border of hysteria.

"I can't tell you anything for the moment. You will have your answers later, ma'am," he said.

The car pulled out at the heliport, a place that Cecilia knew very well. Smith jumped out of the car. "Keep an eye on her, Fox" he reiterated shutting the front door of the car, and approached the policemen standing next to a white Agusta Westland AW139 chopper, ready to lift off.

Fox watched Cecilia crying desperately next to him in the back seat. Handkerchief he took out from his pocket a tissue and handed it to the girl. She was a beautiful woman and his heart melted seeing her crying like that.

"Why?" she sobbed looking straight into his eyes. Her question remained suspended in thin-air without him answering. In that moment Smith made a signal to Fox.

"Come on Mrs. Mendoza." He cheered her on, as a Monegasque policeman opened the door for them. "Let's go!"

"Let's go? Where do we go?" she asked sobbing.

"Don't ask questions, ma'am. Get down from the car and shut up!" Smith approached the car waiting for her to step out.

"I'm a Monegasque citizen, you have no authority to do this to me!" she tried to rebel.

Here we go! The usual rich people who think they always have a solution to all their problems!

"I'm sorry, ma'am, it's the procedure." The monegasque cop handcuffed her.

Now you are speechless, bitch! Smith couldn't refrain from smiling to himself.

Cecilia felt like she was in a movie.

"Take her to the chop!" Smith ordered.

"Why?" She insisted.

Smith snorted. *This woman is truly a pain in the ass. Poor husband of her.*

"Fuck you lady! Stop asking questions!" Smith had lost his patience.

"Okay, okay," she relaxed, approaching the helicopter on her own. She sat in the middle seat. Her face was red like a pepper after crying so much. Her makeup had drained into horrible black lines that decorated her whole face.

"Blindfold her!" Smith ordered Fox, who came up with the black bandana in his hand.

"No, I don't want to! Leave me! Why are you doing this to me?" Cecilia protested "I don't want to, please!"

"Please! Try to be collaborative, Mrs." Fox explained to her. "You have to do exactly what we tell you to do. If you don't cooperate, we will pursue you for obstruction of justice," he said imperatively "Your position would be aggravated and we don't want this, do we?" Fox thought he was talking to his six-year-old daughter.

"All right. I understand, if it's really necessary to blindfold me then do it". Cecilia tried to do her best to be collaborative under those circumstances. A minute later, the chopper hovered like a large dragonfly in the sky. The noise of the propellers was covered by the headphones that Fox had covered her ears with. Alone with your thoughts, Cecilia tried to guess where they were heading. Without seeing anything, it was not possible for her to orientate.

"Who knows what the fuck that stupid husband of mine has done!" Mortified and afraid, she began to address her prayers to Santa Ávila, the only figure who gave her a little consolation and serenity. When the chopper finally began its descend, Cecilia's heart began to beat faster. The instant they landed on the ground, the blood froze in her veins. Fox took off the headphones from her head but not the bandage from her eyes.

"Here we are, *madame.* Don't move until I tell you to."

Cecilia nodded. Fox walked around the helicopter and opened the door on her side, helping her out. "Step down please." He held her by the arm. Cecilia was increasingly scared. Why couldn't she see where they'd brought her?

A door in front of them opened and Cecilia started recognize the sound of her footsteps ticking on the stone floor. The cold shook her up, making her shake. The agents escorted her into an elevator, then walked her down a very long corridor where she heard some voices. Later they made her sit in a room where, once seated, they took off her bandage. Her eyes frowned adapting to the cold ambient light, as she looked around her, she recognised she was in a cold and inhospitable interrogation room; exactly like those she'd seen on television. The agent stood before her. He was holding a folder full of papers. What could have been written in those documents was what most worried Cecilia.

"Mrs. Mendoza. Do you know why you're here?" his voice was cold and dry.

"No" she confessed trying to relax to look more natural.

"No!?" He put her under pressure.

"I guess I'm here because of what my husband did" obviously.

"Then you'll be surprised to know that's not the reason!" His tone was icy.

"No!!??" Cecilia's heart had skipped a beat. She tried to calm down and regain control of herself. She had to remain calm.

"Mrs. Mendoza. The reason why you are here today has nothing to do with your husband" he looked through the file

"Your husband was born in Tennessee on December 2, 1966. He studied finance at Harvard, and climbed the US financial markets. The Financial Times considers him to be the new wolf of Wall Street. He drives a black Maserati, which license plate he changed into DEVIL, plays tennis every Thursday, he's a member of the New York arts club, lives with you on Park Avenue, and has various affairs about which, I suppose, you already know all about it." He paused looking into Cecilia's terrified eyes, who, were in desperate search for an answer.

"I will also tell you, that your husband has committed insider trading. And that's why the SEC keeps a watchful eye on him."

Cecilia turned her gaze. "I don't know anything about this-"

"-shut up! I ask the questions here!" he cut her off abruptly. "As you can see, we know all about you, even what color are the panties you are wearing today."

Cecilia started to cry "What do you want from me? I do not know nothing I don't even know what this SEC is!" she took her face in her hands sobbing desperately.

"SEC stands for Security and Exchange Commission, it's an agency that enforces and regulates the stock market. Anyway that's not the point ma'am. As I said, we are not here for your husband. We are here because we need your help." Cecilia looked at him in amazement "you need my help?"

In that precise moment an American federal agent entered the room "My name is Mulligan. I'm a CIA agent."

"CIA?!" Cecilia cried out incredulously. Mulligan took a chair and sat opposite to her on the other side of the table.

"The reason why you are here is very simple. The US Government wants to infiltrate you into a secret mission that will take place in Venezuela," he explained.

"What? Seriously?" Cecilia passed out in one.

"Seriously. We need someone who can go undercover into the life of the Venezuelan President to facilitate some information, let's say." Added the man.

"You need a bait!" Cecilia murmured.

"We prefer the term infiltrator, m'am," Mulligan pointed out. Cecilia covered her eyes with both hands. "Why me?"

"Before you, we infiltrated other agents, but there is someone close to the President, a spy that we cannot identify yet and we need an outsider, someone who is above suspicion. Someone who is not perceived as a potential danger.

Someone who is Venezuelan and who is a brand image of his country. Just like you."

"Me? But what can I do?"

The agents exchange a foxy glance "The Venezuelan President likes beautiful and successful women. Google's algorithm has shown us that 90% of the times the President has watched pornographic material online, the girl in the videos was a brunette looking like you."

Cecilia blinked her tired, stunned eyes.

"We also found that, of all the images of women with whom we have bombed him in recent months, he clicked with greater propensity on yours." To Cecilia this did not seem like a good news.

"But what do I have to do with all of this? I don't know the President!" she pleaded her cause. The gentlemen in front of her exchanged another complice look.

"We know you don't know him. Now let's go through our plan. You are our infiltrated person, we put you in the President's lap so that you can get as close as possible to him" he explained as if this was absolutely normal "The President will surely notice you, and will want to spend some time alone in your company. This will allow us to carry out our plan, without anyone interfering"

"What are you babbling about?" she was surprised as he felt the blood rumbling in her temples.

"We have a trusted agent in Venezuela, General Miranda. A man straightforward. A real soldier. Thanks to recent developments, Miranda has managed to get close enough to the President. You see this is how it works: you have the loyalists and then there are the second ranking ones. The loyalists are those the President trusts without any reluctance. People upon whom he relies and with whom he shares his secrets, and with whom he decides the direction of the country. Those people have important tasks and control everything.

Then you have people like Miranda, a poor devil who made his career in peripheral regions of the country. People like him never have a chance to remain alone with the President and decide nothing, they just obey orders. However, he has some inputs as well as some relevant information," he explained in detail.

"But what am I supposed to do?" Cecilia whose head was about to explode, complained.

Mulligan looked at her straight in the eyes "You must become the President's lover"

"What? Are you kidding me!?

Get me out of this nightmare, now!

Mulligan who worked at the CIA long enough, was prepared for the desperate reactions of civilians when it was explained to them that they had to act as baits. "In exchange for your cooperation, the American Government will be very generous to you, lady," he smiled.

"I do not care! I do not want to!" She resisted.

Look at this little bitch. How temperamental she is, he thought as he opened the file on the table. "Let's see ... your husband has violated the American financial security code twice, plus you have not declared taxes for 2018, and have not issued an invoice for a photo shooting you did back in..."

"All right! I get it! I have to collaborate, yes or yes." She sighed.

"As said it would be easier for everyone if you cooperated, madame. Think about your husband-"

"-fuck my husband!" She roared, crossing her arms on her chest. On a second thought if Tom's bank accounts were to be frozen, she too would have been left with no money. Their prenuptial contract would had melted like snow in the sun. "Where's Tom?" She asked, "In our custody until the mission is accomplished," Mulligan simply said.

"So you put him in jail?" She said.

"Unfortunately it was necessary to secure your collaboration," he commented without taking his eyes off the papers he was inspecting.

Cecilia took a deep breath "Oh well. At this point what do you want me to do? I don't think I have been left many options, she sighted to herself.

"Indeed there are none," the agent stated. "In exchange for your collaboration, we will make disappear all your family's little felonies."

"Provided that I won't be killed in the meantime," Cecilia exclaimed.

"Not gonna happen. We are the CIA, we have experience in the matter."

"Yes I can totally see that. That's why you need a Miss to help you out in such a complicated case," she mocked them.

"I advise you to keep your judgments to yourself" Mulligan's gaze was serious. Cecilia stretched on the chair. If she had to dance, she would have danced, but at least she would have chosen the music. "I understand" she added "but in return I want, please write it down: I don't want to pay taxes for the rest of my life, I want an apartment on Fifth Avenue in New York, my mother and sister to become American citizens and move to Miami. I also want an amount of money corresponding to 20 million dollars to be deposited into a bank account in my name only. And then I also want to be the leading actress in the next Hollywood hit of the year!" Mulligan and the others exchanged a questioning look. "By any chance, wouldn't you also like to become the President of the United States? Why not?!" Everyone laughed.

"Look, I'm not kidding. You need me, I don't need you." She challenged them with a glance in her eyes. "The Government is willing to give you an economic compensation of 10 million dollars"

Cecilia laughed. "Do you really think that for that ridiculous amount of money, I would betray my homeland? I am married to a millionaire. Don't make me waste my time, please!" She left everyone in the room speechless.

"All right. I'm going to make a phone call." Mulligan disappeared behind a fake mirror.

"It's a tough nut to crack," he said to his boss on the phone.

On the other end of the receiver, Carter played with a pen in his office. "Give her what she wants. We have already failed three times, we have no other choice."

"All right, sir," Mulligan replied respectfully. The shit must have hit the fan if Carter had agreed so easily. "Make sure she's well prepared."

"Yes, sir. Today we start training."

"All right. There is no time to waste" he hanged up.

Mulligan went back to the other room. "All right Barbie. You won 20 million bucks. Now follow me. We have a lot of work to do."

CHAPTER 8

Caracas

Seated in her penthouse in the luxurious Altamira building, Cecilia watched from the imposing stained-glass window, the most beautiful square in the capital spread out before her eyes. In the past two months her life had changed completely. The frenzied shopping sessions had left room for meetings on the situation in her country and on the habits of the President Fernando Rodríguez. Such a treacherous and insensitive President, who'd let Venezuela in the hands of drug trafficking, and people starve, and corruption spread everywhere.

"A country without a future" these were the words Mulligan had said to her and which now rang in her head. Even though she had money now, Cecilia remembers how hard it was to live in Venezuela. The sacrifices her mom had made to make sure she could achieve her dreams.

"After all, nothing ever changes in this country," she recalled her mother's words. A simple but very wise woman. Lately she often happened to think about her and her sister hidden, who knows where, under a false identity outside of the country. Mulligan had explained to her that it was essential to put her family under protection.

"May the will of God be done," Cecilia'd said. She was already half accustomed to this strange situation she was in.

Cecilia turned on the bath tap and let the water run. She got undressed in front of the mirror analyzing her body step by step. She was still young and had a magnificent body. She noticed that it hadn't changed at all in the last few years, also thanks to the constant aesthetic treatments she was undergoing. When the water reached the edge of the tub, Cecilia lit candles and relaxed in the hot water.

She tried to get the stress out of her body. Finally, the evening had come when she would meet the President. She came prepared. The Orinoco Operation was officially about to begin.

At nineteen hours sharp the car came to pick her up. She went down looking at her figure in the elevator mirror, as beautiful as always. General Miranda waited on the sidewalk. When he saw her, he immediately opened the large glass door of the entrance for her. "Ms. Mendoza, it's a pleasure to meet you!" He said, being almost enchanted by her beauty.

"My pleasure" she smiled, stretching her hand towards him and immediately noticing that Miranda was foaming at the mouth. "I'm General Miranda. Nice to finally meet you, I have heard a lot about you. Please come in." He pointed to the car and opened the door for her. Cecilia sat in the comfortable cockpit, while Miranda walked around to sit next to her. "We can talk freely, Miss," he said, eyeing the driver who started the car.

"Do you have any questions?"

"No. I'd rather know something about yourself."

"I am a General. I have spent most of my career in the Amazon region and Bolívar state. At that time, I was involved in mining. As you know, there are many mines, and great interests of international corporations"

"How did you meet Mulligan?"

"Let's see ... I met him many years ago, when I worked in the mining region. Many American companies had contracts with our Government to guarantee stability to the United

States. Then things started to go wrong when Rodríguez became President. It was at that moment when Mulligan told me that the situation was no longer sustainable. It was at that point that they decided to invest to keep this country from going, sorry, to shit." Cecilia listened attentively, so he continued "the Operation Orinoco aimed at defenestrating President Rodríguez began then. It was a disaster. The President knew it and cut all contacts with foreign companies, accusing the Americans of colonialism. It was the first wave of the Venezuelan Grand Nationalizations. The CIA set in motion a second Orinoco Operation, but that too was a disaster. The President had become even more firm in his positions and took advantage of the opportunity to nationalize the little that still remained of private. As you see, this is the result," he concluded, looking out the window at the city of Caracas which had become the ghost of itself.

Cecilia gave him a deep look, *who knows what Mulligan promised you* she thought.

"Mulligan gave me the same picture of the situation." She said.

The General thought that Cecilia looked way younger than in the pictures. She was also much more beautiful, as her features were more delicate. However, he still wasn't entirely convinced that a girl like her could actually accomplish such a delicate mission.

"Why do you think the other operations went wrong?" Cecilia asked seriously. Miranda frowned "The President is very cautious. He knows he has enemies, that's why you have to infiltrate unsuspected people, just like you. Service agents are easy to spot. We shall bear in mind that Rodríguez is not only a General himself, but keeps very close ties with all intelligence services in a variety of foreign countries. Those services are the ones who pass on the information to him. So, I would say that the winning solution is to look outside of the small circle, for undercover missions." The General looked out. "We are almost there". Cecilia recognized the Miraflores Government building, which she had seen on television many times. "It's awesome!"

"Yes. Especially when compared to the disaster of the city. Don't be impressed, you will see everything in there, get ready" he said, adjusting his jacket. "Ready?" Chucked

She was God damns ready. She had spent weeks anxiously awaiting for this moment. The driver stopped in front of the military guards located at the entrance.

"Good evening" he said lowering the glass. "I'm General Miranda and Mrs. Mendoza." A soldier checked with the mirror under the car and inspected the trunk before letting them through. The car paraded through the huge tropical gardens and, a few minutes later, stopped in front of the palace entrance. Two policemen opened both doors of the car and escorted them inside. Cecilia felt excited. Inside the venue, dozens of people dressed in uniforms chatted among themselves while sipping champagne. The few women wore colorful clothes of famous European brands, which were lovely.

"Welcome General," said one of the guests approaching towards them.

"Governor! What a pleasure to see you again! May I introduce Miss Universe, our beauty queen Cecilia Mendoza"

"Nice to meet you. You are one of the international ambassadors of this country" Miss Cecilia thanked him with a smile. "He is the Governor of the Sucre State," added Miranda.

"Shall we proceed to the bar?" The Governor wanted to have a drink.

"Sure. I was just looking for it. How are things going, Governor?" he asked.

"Well, I'm looking into some relief programs for the poor.

Poverty is a widespread problem in our region. Especially now that there is no tourism. It's very sad. People suffer a lot, we are intervening massively". Cecilia thought about how badly her compatriots were doing. Miranda ordered a glass of something. "Yes I know. But our President is very focused on facilitating access to credit for the poorest. "Obviously. But due to the continuing devaluation of our currency the situation is not ideal. What would you like to drink Miss?" He asked.

"Champagne," she replied.

"Three glasses of champagne, please," he said to the waiter. "And you Ms. Mendoza, when have you been crowned?"

"In 2013 I won the national pageant and the following year I became Miss Universe"

"A title that you absolutely deserve!" he smiled at her "do you live in Caracas?"

"Back and forth. I have some job contracts with fashion houses in New York."

"Obviously it is always better to keep the money you earn outside of this country. We all remember what a disastrous situation happened when the Banco Latino went on bankruptcy," he mentioned. There was no Venezuelan who could not remember when, the bank owner, together with his political friends, ran away with the money of the poor people.

"Yes, it was a very sad page in our history," said Cecilia.

"Good evening, Miranda!" The loyal General Aguirre joined them from behind

"Dear Miguel how are you?"

"Well we managed to stop the riots in the Zulia district. It was a success. We have to toast!"

"What riots?" Cecilia asked.

Aguirre looked her up and down "Who is she?"

"Sorry! I haven't introduced you! Cecilia Mendoza Miss Universe. General Aguirre" Miranda introduced them.

"Delighted," said Aguirre, kissing her hand as he pictured in his mind Miranda fucking her. A very unattractive view, he had to admit to himself.

"There have been some public unrest. Demonstrations against the President, but don't worry Miss, we have put them back in their place," he grinned.

"There have been a lot of riots lately. It's all the fault of the Americans who don't want to buy our oil," explained Miranda.

"Americans are absolute evil" Aguirre began to stick his index finger in the air so that people would pay more attention to what he was saying "we must fight against them to maintain control of our country. "Long live our President and long live the Bolivarian socialist revolution!" he raised his glass in the air.

"Viva!" the whole room exploded.

"Ladies and gentleman" a voice on the microphone began to speak "please come to the entrance. Our most excellent President and head of the Socialist Bolivarian Republic of Venezuela, Fernando Rodríguez, welcomes you!" In an explosion of noisemakers, the President leaned over the balustrade and started descending the stairs triumphantly. Fernando Rodríguez was born 44 years earlier in a town on the coast of Venezuela, on the Caribbean Sea. His father worked occasionally and his family was so poor that Fernando and his four brothers had not been able to study. They spent time selling shell necklaces on the street and had learned to read thanks to a neighbor. Already as a child, Fernando, who was the younger of his brothers, showed leadership and toughness. Years later, thanks to the priest of his town, Fernando managed to enter the military school of Caracas. A tough man, with few friends, a passion for power. He had worked on various positions before founding a political party inspired by radical Marxism.

"People take control" was the slogan that had raged in a poor country like Venezuela. As time went by, his military career had led him to enter the restricted circle of President Oriondo, his predecessor. It was from there that he managed to organize a Bolivarian Marxist *coup d'état.*

He raised the people and the military against Oriondo.

"You, one of my faithful Generals!" It'd been President Oriondo's last words.

"I am not faithful to anyone but myself!" Fernando had confessed moments before killing him. "May his body never be found again" he had ordered his soldiers who threw the body into the waters of the Orinoco where the piranhas made it disappear in less than a minute. In his first TV speech that evening, Rodríguez said that the enemy Oriondo had fled to the US with American collaboration, and brought the country's gold reserves with him. In front of all the networks and his compatriots Rodrìguez had said "It is with great sadness that I communicate that President Oriondo, faced with the political unrest that is taking place across the country, has decided to resort to the protection of our enemy number one: the United States of America. It will be my job to take the steering wheel of this wonderful country in my hands, to ensure a worthy future for our people and the millions of Venezuelans who work honestly." That was the moment when he had proclaimed himself President of Venezuela.

That evening the President went down the stairs in his military uniform. He was immediately struck by a beautiful brunette girl. Her name was Cecilia Mendoza. Without waiting too long, he walked towards her, silencing all those who in the meantime approached him to pay their respects to him. "Finally a beautiful girl!" Fernando said to Cecilia.

"I am honored to meet you Mr. President!"

"Is she with you?" He turned to Miranda who nodded

"She is one of us"

"You are very bad, Miranda. How did you keep such a beautiful creature from me? I'm going to have to get you arrested!"

"The President always knows how to be funny," chanted Miranda.

"What's your name?"

"Cecilia, Cecilia Mendoza" she stared at him with that sort of pride that only woman who came from below as she, could have.

"What a beautiful name" Rodríguez was enraptured by that creature and could not take his eyes off her.

"The most beautiful woman in the world for the most important President in the world" Miranda gloated, making him return to himself.

"Miss Mendoza," said Rodríguez, "I would be glad to invite you to lunch tomorrow, you and I alone." Exactly what Mulligan and his algorithm had predicted.

"Mr. President! It would be an honor for me!" she faked emotion and uncertainty. Miranda felt relieved to see that the situation was going exactly as they had expected. Let's hope Cecilia was really prepared as they reported him.

The President let out a triumphant smile. "Now please Cecilia, stay with me. I want to introduce you to someone." She remained glued to his side during the entire evening, she let people speak to her, and smiled as if she were on Miss Universe's podium again.

In those moments Miranda found that men are very stupid in front of female beauty. He, who was a straight forward General, would never fall for a charade like this. "One shall only hope that this will work" he thought sipping his glass of champagne. "To Venezuela to my homeland and to Simon Bolívar" he cheered to himself.

Across the room, Cecilia was amazed by the luxury of the building and how quietly these people talked about golf, while the country was ravaged and Venezuelians were starving. While there was a curfew on the streets, those politicians eat caviar and champagne which, by the way, were under embargo. In the end she, who in her life always was interested only in fashion magazines and herself, and who had accepted this assignment only because they had forced her, was almost proud to be able to contribute to the restoration of justice in her land. After several tedious speeches, the President was all eyes only for his next conquest. "Where do you live Cecilia?" he just couldn't take his eyes off those curves.

"Between here and Montecarlo"

"Really? I like Montecarlo"

"Have you been there President?" She fooled around a bit.

"Obviously! I have a house in Montecarlo" he said as if it was normal "In fact, I have houses scattered a bit across the world"

Cecilia smiled dwelling into her "MISS mode" pretending to be naive, false and that she had only being aiming at him for power and money. This, after all, was what any other woman in her place would have done. She aggressively flirted with him while rubbing his hand and getting very close. "President, you are so ... smart!"

Rodríguez was completely enchanted by this creature "I like being with you, stay here tonight" he whispered in her ear.

"But what am I going to tell to Miranda?"

"I am the President. I don't have to justify myself," he said. Then he thought better not to rush. After all a little background search on this woman would had been helping before letting her into his bed. "You're right. There are too many people here tonight."

"I will see you tomorrow, Mr. President. I will count the

minutes until then ..." she bit her lip.

"Call me Fernando. See you tomorrow"

"Shall I leave my number to you?"

"We will find it, don't worry."

His eyes followed Cecilia walking towards Miranda. He made a hand gesture to his Minister of Interiors. "Cardoza! Come here. Have you seen that girl? Well, I want to know everything about her including whether she dyes her hair or not, understand?"

"Yes sir" Cardoza was used to not asking questions when it came to run some background check-in the many girls that frequented Rodríguez's bedroom.

Cecilia and Miranda got into the car. "How did I go?" she asked apprehensively.

"Very good!" the General commented "I didn't think, frankly, that it would be so simple".

Cecilia wondered if it was possible that an algorithm could know a person better than a human. Apparently it was.

"Incredible! In one night, you managed to do way more than what others have taken years." Miranda was ecstatic.

"How much do they give you, General?" Cecilia could not keep her forked tongue from asking.

"Say again??"

"I asked you how much money do the Americans pay you to do all this?"

Miranda could not believe it. "Cecilia do you realize that I am a Venezuelan General. My job is to give my life for my country if necessary. Do you really see me as a traitor to my homeland?"

She peered at him silently.

"I'm not the man you think! Maybe you think so because you are young. But just so you know money is not everything in this life. There is another thing worth dying for: honor.

Cecilia realized in that moment how inappropriate her question was.

"I know the world goes somewhere else. But I'm an idealist and I firmly believe that I'm doing the right thing. Pull over here please!" he said to the driver. "Come down, Cecilia!" he barked as the car pulled up. The girl was shaken by shivers. "What are you doing, are you crazy? Won't you leave me here alone at night?"

"Silly, I won't leave you here! My God, who do you think I am? I want you to come and see for yourself. Look! Look at Venezuela square." They both got out of the car, the General held her hand firmly. They arrived near the fountain, right in the center of the square. The car was stopped on one side.

"Look. There aren't even any lightbulbs left. People steal them because they no longer know what to steal to eat!" Cecilia's dress fluttered in the air, while the water from the fountain lightly splashed on her bare arms. Cecilia understood what he was saying.

"See Cecilia. This is how our Venezuela has become. Frankly, I am ashamed of it because I am a General, and I feel responsible for it."

"I understand," she replied, digging into that man's desperate eyes.

"Come on, let's go back to the car. Before they kidnap us." As they got on board the car started towards Plaza Altamira, gliding through a city that looked more and more the specter of itself.

CHAPTER 9

Miraflores

Half an hour later, Cardoza knocked on Rodríguez's door. "Come in! Ah, Cardoza, I was just waiting for you. Tell me, what did you find out?" The man approached the President closing the door behind him. "Nothing special Mr. President. She was born in the Coche district, she is 27 years old, we do not even know who her father is. Not that this matters as he disappeared in the 90's, probably run off to Colombia, anyway there is no trace of him. Cecilia and her sister are registered under the surname of their mom, Mendoza. Her mother has always worked as a cleaning lady. She even worked for an English family in El Rosal. When they left to go back to Europe she found herself unemployed. Everything she earned she had invested it into turning her daughter into a beauty queen."

"What else?" seated in the large armchair, the President propped his fingertips of both hands between them.

"I spoke with the Dream House." They said that Cecilia was an excellent student and that she wanted to become a Miss at all costs. Her family had no money and for her it was a form of social redemption. The girl was very tenacious and moved by a strong ambition absolutely out of the ordinary."

"It doesn't surprise me. All of us who come from nothing have it. Tell me Cardoza, do you know who she voted for?"

"Yes, it says here that they have voted for the Bolivarian party. That means she voted for you in the last elections."

"Well, we all know that those elections were rigged. The whole country voted for me. However, I am happy to know that in principle she voted for me. One last thing" he added "Is she married?"

"No" Cardoza said.

Perfect Rodríguez thought.

CHAPTER 10

Altamira building

Cecilia couldn't sleep that night. How could all this has happened? Her life was perfect in the monotony of wealth she now regretted. What a mess! And what would had she say to the President? She had come to senses with the idea of having to go to bed with him. Back at CIA they had explained this topic to her very clearly. "You will have to become his friend. His close friend."

The President liked beautiful women, like her. But he was also the type of man who would easily turn uninterested, so she would have to implement the plan as quick as possible.

"Thank goodness he is not ugly," she'd commented during the training, making Mulligan run his fingers through his hair. The truth being he was a much more handsome man in person than he appeared in the photos. On the other hand, people used to say to her that she as well looked younger in person. Rodríguez was tall and robust; he looked more like a Hollywood actor than an evil President. He didn't really had the face for that role. He would had been perfect to script in the role of a charming Latin James Bond. Anyway she thought that the fact that she did not find him repugnant, would have contributed to make the whole charade more natural. At 12 sharp the following day, Cecilia passed through the doors of Presidencial La Casona Residence. A less opulent mansion than Miraflores. It was a very simple Spanish-style house with white walls and wooden roofs. A very peaceful environment in which she immediately felt at ease.

"Miss Mendoza" a guard welcomed her. "Follow me, please. The President will be with you in a minute." He showed her the large armchairs on the patio which was lushing with tropical flowers. In her white lace dress combined with a hat, Cecilia sat down with her long legs crossed. She asked for a Coca-Cola Light to the attendant who came to see what she wanted to drink. Beautiful scarlet macaw parrots got on a tree in the garden, croaking excitedly. *I'm finally home,* she told herself. Those childhood memories resurfaced in her mind. When as a child she wanted to do like these parrots: fly away from misery, in the blue sky.

"Cecilia! I am very glad that you accepted my invitation." The President's voice dissolved her thoughts. He approached her and got once again amazed by her beauty, which the daylight had not altered from the previous evening.

Cecilia shrugged "For me it's an honor, Mr. President"

"How many times shall I tell you to call me Fernando. For you, I am Fernando, and not the President," he said sympathetically.

"All right!" Cecilia put a hand on her chest as if to apologize.

"Don't worry, honey. Sit down. Make yourself comfortable. I want to know everything about you." He pretended not to know everything about her already.

"Actually I don't have a very interesting life like yours," she caressed his hand.

"My? For God's sake, it's more boring than it seems, believe me! But I'm more interested in knowing yours," he insisted, taking a *tequeño* from the plate.

"I'm from Caracas. I grew up in the Coche Urbanization, where I lived with my mother and sister. My father abandoned us when we were very young and from that moment onwards it was my mother who took care of us" she began to explain.

"What job did your mother do?"

"She was a cleaning lady. But one day they robbed the bus she was traveling on and broke her arm. To stole her bag, you know? So she has been out of work for a long time. Luckily there were social aid programs, otherwise we would literally starve." She dropped it knowing that Fernando would like the subtle reference to the social programs he was so fond of. In reaction he smiled "I always said that the social plan had to be the pillar of this society. The first part to be implemented and expanded just after the Bolivarian revolution. Did you and your sister study?"

"Yes, we studied at the Dolores Mission, a Catholic Institute. Then my mother thought I might have some chance of becoming a beauty queen, and so she enrolled me at the House of Dreams where I passed the selections" exactly as the CIA psychologist had told her, she was about to get emotional. A move that would have triggered in him, the unconscious will to protect her.

"And you did it!" He put a hand on her knee.

Cecilia smiled "it was a dream for me."

"I like your story; it is very similar to mine. Because in life it's not important where you come from-"

"But where do you want to go!" she spoked over him.

"Exactly! You read my thought. Rodríguez made a pause thinking that determination was the only card to play to go on in life when you came from nothing like them. "Well. Cecilia aren't you wondering why I have invited you over today?".

"What if I said that the answer is no?" she dared to say taking a sip of her cola. Fernando chuckled "You are a fascinating creature, Cecilia"

"Because you don't know me well yet," she said sighing to pull her chest out. She knew that he could had not prevented to give a good look at her tits.

"Don't worry, I won't let you go until I know everything about you." Cecilia wedged her eyes into his and thought that until now it was going as planned. At that precise moment a waiter came to say that lunch was served.

They ate in the patio, surrounded by singing parrots and squeaking birds. Occasionally some General would interrupt them to whisper some emergency in Rodríguez's ear. Fernando gave them orders to do this, this, that, and then lovingly returned to turn his attention to Cecilia. Whenever she saw a General approaching, Cecilia's heart skipped a beat thinking that her cover had blown. Even if she didn't show it, she was quite nervous, although Doctor Fliss' pills were casting their effect.

Fernando had noticed that, although she simulated well, the girl was nervous; which seemed normal to him, since she was in the presence of the President. After lunch, Fernando showed her the sumptuous tropical gardens and the interior of the residence. He took Cecilia by the hands and kissed her intensely. Cecilia didn't expect it to be so impetuous, but let him do it. A long, sexy, determined and stubborn kiss. Just like him. She thought it would not be easy for her to entertain such a man in the bedroom.

"Come with me," he said, leading her directly to his room. Cecilia entered the room and felt a little un-eased as she didn't know where she was going to.

"It's very simple here," she stated, looking around when she realized that he had brought her straight to his master bedroom.

Her eyes dwelled around in search of some information about him. There was nothing relevant. Everything was normal and tidy. After all, Fernando was a soldier.

"That's how I like it: Simple" he sat on the bed edge. He lifted the telephone receiver "Dolores? I don't want to be disturbed for an hour. For no reason, understood?" He instructed his secretary, then hanged up the receiver and exhaled deeply. "Well? What are you waiting for?" he said undoing his shirt.

CHAPTER 11

Washington

Agent Mulligan arrived early at his office that morning. He took his usual macchiato with two lumps of sugar that his secretary brought him as a daily routine.

He glanced at the emails he had received. As always, he was bombarded with emergencies to which he should have responded right away. While replying to the first email of the morning, the phone rang.

"Mulligan," he said.

"It's Miranda," said the voice on the other end of the phoneline.

"How are things going on so far?" he stretched his legs and rested his feet on the desk.

"Well. The letter is in his hands" that was the secret code to say that Cecilia was with the President. Cecilia *was* the letter.

"And what did he say when he received it?"

"He was happy. Now let's wait and hope that the girl knows what to do." Mulligan's voice exuded a strong concern.

"Are you worried, General?" he asked.

"Yes. As long as the missions isn't over I'm always nervous," he explained.

"Relax, it's the best thing to do under these circumstances." Miranda's tone continued to indicate concern.

"You know. It's not the first time we've done this sort of

things," he tried to calm him down. He knew how dangerous it was when someone started showing signs of imbalance during a mission.

"I know. But I'm afraid for the girl. She is not an expert and she is a civilian. The others, before her, were prepared."

Did Miranda really care about her? Was he going completely nuts, or what?

"Don't worry. She knows what she is doing," he added dryly, "thank you for the call, don't worry, everything will be fine" and he hanged down.

"Hopefully" Miranda hung up the phone and wiped the sweat away from his forehead with a tissue. That night he'd dreamed that Cecilia cover had blown and the police tortured her upon Rodrìguez request. She had blurted out everything. *It's just a bad dream, you really need to calm down*, he told himself. He was obviously under a huge stress for he knew that in case something went wrong, his head would be the first one in rolling.

CHAPTER 12

Caracas

3315 km south, Cecilia had returned to her home in Plaza Altamira. As the elevator doors opened directly into her exquisite art deco penthouse, she took off her stilettos. The President have had what he wanted, now it was her turn to make sure that he didn't lose interest on her.

One month left. I have to cope with this for only a month, she thought. That was the duration of the Orinoco Operation. As expected, Fernando had proven to be impetuous and determined in bed. Someone who knew what he wanted and wanted it now. Although she would have preferred to keep the charade up for a little longer in order to make their relationship grow solid before ending up in bed with him, she hadn't have much of a choice. If it had been easy for her to win the earth of an American, thanks to the fact that the Yankees went crazy for exotic latinas, to conquer Fernando was a much more demanding task as he was used to girls like her. He would not have easily fallen into her charme and that is why Cecilia had now to think on how to let him fall into her trap. She couldn't afford the luxury of him losing interest in her. And she knew those things could happen, as it already happened with her husband Tom.

I can't set a foot wrong.

She sat down on the sofa; alone with her thoughts. *What shall I do if you don't call me?* An idea flashed through her mind but it was too risky. She fantasied over the sex they had that afternoon. Although she didn't want to, she had to admit that they both had a lot of fun. She would have never guessed; even though she always liked men who knew exactly what they wanted. She was surprised that on contrary of what she'd expected, he'd been attentive to her needs too. Now, that she was thinking about how she could had handled the situation in case he wouldn't call her back, the phone rang. It was Fernando calling from his private cell phone.

"Cecilia, honey," he said as Cecilia heaved a sigh of relief. She'd never waited with such trepidation for a guy to call.

"Hi Fernando, how was your day?"

"Good. I wanted to know how are you?"

"Very well, after spending the afternoon with you," he smiled as the image of the sex marathon they had popped out in his brain.

"I hope I haven't been brusque," he added

"That's how I like it...you know" she flirted, snatching a laugh from him.

"Mmmmm," he said, remembering how soft her skin was. "Are you free tomorrow?"

"I should go shopping, but let's see what do you offer, before taking a decision"

"I have a surprise for you," he said, as Cecilia's blood froze in her veins. Lately the word *surprise* terrified her.

"Let's do this way: I will send you a car at 2 pm sharp so that in the morning you are free to go shopping. By the way I am curious... where are you going?" he was jealous.

"Now you are checking upon me?" she replied in pure South American style.

"Of course. In fact, I would like to point out that from tonight, you do have some company".

"Sorry, I don't understand" she was dumbfounded.

"Check out the window. Have a look at your building entrance."

Cecilia walked quickly towards the entry hall of her apartment, where she approached the impressively large window. She looked down "What exactly am I looking for?" her eyes spotted some cars driving around.

"Do you see two cars? A blue and a white one?"

"Yes" she identified them immediately.

"From now on these cars will follow you wherever you go."

"Oh! Fernando!" She pretended to be pleasantly surprised "all these attentions just for me?"

Shit! How am I supposed to do with Miranda now.

"You shouldn't have, Fernando!"

"Security reasons. I am letting you know so that you don't get scared if you see these two cars following you. You know it's a necessary precaution."

"Thanks for warning me. I can't believe it!" she disguised her desperation under a false enthusiasm.

"This is nothing. You will see. See you tomorrow honey!" Fernando said gently

"I Miss you already," she ended the conversation.

Now, Cecilia was shaking. *How am I supposed to do this?* She was sure she had all conversations intercepted and cameras placed all over her apartment. *Somehow I have to find a way to get in touch with the General.*

Time had come to pay a visit to Agent Maxwell. But how avoiding them to get suspicious? An idea flashed through her mind, it was way too early to be credible, in case she was under track. She decided to wait.

At 7 pm she went to the kitchen and pulled a packet of rice out from the drawers. She took a pot and filled it with water.

"How dumb I am!" she said out loud "I ran out of salt!" She quickly walked towards the elevator and went two stories down where the Alicante family lived. She rang the doorbell while adjusting her hair as she waited. A few seconds later, Agent Maxwell opened the door; the fake maid uniform suited her well.

"Good evening" she pretended not to know her,

"Sorry for the inconvenience, I'm the neighbor upstairs" she smiled "I ran out of salt, wouldn't you be polite enough to give me some?" Agent Maxwell understood immediately.

"Of course Ma'am. Please come in. The Alicante's are not home at the moment. Let me get some salt for you"

"What a lavish apartment," Cecilia exclaimed looking around at the Chinese vases that adorned the entrance. Maxwell did not reply. She went straight to the kitchen and returned with a small pack of salt in her hands. As she took it, Cecilia glided a small piece of paper into the palm of her hand.

"Thank you so much! Good evening"

"Goodbye ma'am" the agent shut the door closed and proceeded immediately to the toilet where she opened the piece of paper:

two cars are watching me in front of the entrance to the house. Tomorrow I'll see the President again, I will get in touch when I can.

She threw the paper it in the toilet and flushed it down.

At least I have managed to solve one problem, Cecilia thought while heading back to her apartment, where she cooked some rice and went to sleep after saying her prayers.

The next day at 2 pm, the driver came to pick her up. As soon as she got in, the car immediately moved towards the exact opposite direction from La Casona.

"Excuse me, where are we going?" Cecilia looked out worried.

"I have precise instructions not to tell you, ma'am. However, it is not in La Casona that I am driving you to" he glanced at her in the rearview mirror.

Enough with all these surprises! she sagged on the seat.

Driving around the streets of Caracas, Cecilia found it hard to recognize her city. The modern buildings which at the time were shiny brand new, now appeared like if they have been blowed out in an explosion. Groups of poor people wandered around the streets carrying machine guns. The shopping windows of the few shops left, were broken and the beautiful fountains that adorned the squares were turned off waterless. The dirt increased, so did the size of the slums *or ranchos* as they were called in Venezuela. Everything seemed ugly and dirty. Only nature was beautiful as always and impressive as she remembered.

The car turned in front of a military garrison. "We're here ma'am"

"Are you sure?" she asked lowering the window by only two fingers.

"Absolutely. The President is waiting for you here." Cecilia tried not to look worried. With great surprise when the car stopped she saw that they were in a military base in the downtown area.

"Miss Mendoza" a soldier approached her as she stepped out of the car "please come this way; the helicopter is ready for takeoff."

"What!? A helicopter !? Why!?" tension increased.

"You'll have to ask that question to the President himself, Miss," replied the soldier. Twenty minutes later Fernando arrived escorted by his guards. He jumped out of the car with the expression on his face indicating he was a tough guy. It was the usual expression he would put on display when he was in front of his militaries.

"Everything ready?" He asked his loyalists.

"Yes, sir".

"All right. Then we are off. Have a nice weekend, everyone" He greeted. Cecilia, who already sat in the helicopter, immediately understood that he would take her somewhere for the weekend. This gave her some relief.

"Hi, honey!" He blew her a kiss as soon as the rotor started to tilt and took off instantly.

"Fernando!" She said in surprise "Where are you taking me?"

"It's surprise and I don't want to spoil it!" he placed the headphones around her ears while as the helicopter started the engines and took off instantly.

"Are you going to tell me where we are going?" She fidgeted into the microphone.

"Don't worry. I'll take you to heaven." He smiled, clenching her hand into his.

CHAPTER 13

Paradise Island.

An hour later, they touched down on a pristine Caribbean island. The fine white sand was wetting into the transparent water. The leaves of the palm trees floated in the air moved by the breeze. Cecilia took a deep breath. Fernando hadn't told her a lie, they were in heaven.

Their minivan proceeded in the middle of the luxuriant nature. There was nothing but tropical plants as far as the eye could see and beautiful colored flowers. Suddenly from a distance, a white house in pure colonial style popped out. A statuesque building with classic iron colonial rails on the windows. A structure that fitted perfectly into the nature of the place. They got out of the car. Cecilia couldn't have expected a bigger surprise than that.

"Where we are?"

"Welcome to my house!" Fernando kissed her hand. Wow! That was unexpected.

"Hi Miguel" Rodríguez greeted the gentleman who approached him in a waiter uniform.

"Good morning, Mr. President"

"Good morning!" a lady who Cecilia thought was the housekeeper smiled at her in welcome.

"Relax, honey. You'll like being here," Fernando whispered.

"Please, Miss. I'll show you to your room," said the housekeeper, climbing the terracotta stairs. Cecilia could not believe it! Was this his home? The paladin of the citizens' house? Really? She rolled her eyes around her. It must have been a very old house, at least so it seemed.

"It's an historic building, you know?" The housekeeper said "My name is Milly. It would actually be Milagros, but you can call me Milly," she added smiling.

"I'm Cecilia nice to meet you."

"I know! You are a beauty queen, that's like being a goddess for us Venezuelans! It is a pride to have you here with us." Cecilia smiled awkwardly "Is this an historic building?"

"Indeed! It is an ancient sugar *hacienda*, or factory. There are thousands of hectares of land." She emphasized her words with broad gestures of her hands. "Don't you believe me?" She added staring at Cecilia's lost expression "then come with me! I'll show you" Milly left the Miss suitcases on the first floor right in front of the door of her room and carried her through a series of rooms, until they came out on a large terrace that dominated the natural luxuriant nature to the crystal clear sea. "Here it is. All your eyes can see is property of this hacienda. Cecilia was impressed by the vastness of the place.

"Wow! How beautiful! I wouldn't have expected it to be so big"

"Didn't he tell you?" Asked Milly.

"What didn't he tell me?" She was very lost

"That the island is its own. Of the President, I mean. It belongs to him. All here is his. Beaches, restaurants, bars. Even the ground where the churches are built!"

"What?!"

"I swear!" Milly was thrilled. "Now, come. I'll take you to your room".

Fifteen minutes later, Cecilia still couldn't believe it. Lying in the beautiful canopy bed, she looked out of the window in disbelief. The large white curtains danced in the wind. Like the ideas in her head. She closed her eyes for a moment. Everything was a hoax then. Populism, this fantastic illusion that she too had believed in as a young woman, was only a fantasy. A system by which people were led to think that we are all equal, while everyone has his own interests; especially those who commanded. *That's how the world goes*, she thought. She got up and looked at the beautiful room furnished with traditional objects and paintings from the Amazonian tribes hanging on the white walls. In the bathroom there were several beauty products still in their packaging and many relaxing candles. Again, she found it hard to believe she was there. She wondered where Fernando was; and where Miranda must have been. *Will Miranda know that I'm here?* Many questions that remained unanswered. Someone knocked on the door.

"Miss Mendoza" Milly's voice asked softly. Cecilia replied "Please come in" as she got out of the bed.

"May I?" she said opening the door gently "I would like to show you where you will find everything you need" she walked towards the large built-in wardrobe "Look. Here are some clothes the President made me buy for you. I hope you like them! I chose a little bit of everything to make you feel comfortable" she opened the closet door, revealing clothes of all colors "Did you buy all this for me?" The Miss' eyes stood out of their orbits.

"Yes Madame. As the President instructed me" she winked at her. Milly left saying that the President was currently busy, but that he would wait for Cecilia downstairs for dinner at 8:00 pm. As soon as the housekeeper left, Cecilia inspected it all. There was quite a selection! Full length dresses, lace dresses, evening gowns, day clothes, swimwear, wedges, heeled shoes, colored blouses, lingerie and much more. Everything was from famous bands and the current seasonal collection. Another thing that left her surprised was the high number of pieces. *How long does he wants me to stay here?*

By 8 PM the blue sky had turned to black. Cecilia had prepared herself for dinner. She wore a very simple yellow silk dress, which highlighted her spectacular body and in particular her breast. Leaving the external corridor, a light breeze blew ruffling her hair and amplifying the sound of the sea. Cecilia deeply inhaled that familiar air. It was the smell of her home, her country, her people. The smell of her land Venezuela. She went down the stairs on her golden heels, and walked to the living room. Fernando was there, sitting at the table, talking on the phone. He wore white linen trousers, combined with a shirt of the same color. Cecilia couldn't help but think that he was handsome. She went over to the table and sat down, as if everything was normal.

"Something to drink?" asked the waitress.

Cecilia said no with a single gesture of the hand that Fernando grabbed into his before she lowered back at its place. He kissed her hand tenderly.

"I get it. Yes, we'll talk about it." He ended the conversation and glanced at her from top to bottom. For years he hadn't seen something as beautiful as this woman. "You are jaw dropping Cecilia. You're a goddess, the goddess of beauty," he sighed. She smiled back and he asked her "Do you like this place?"

"It's a paradise."

"Right um? It is my paradise and now our paradise" his chest was filled with pride. "I have a question for you, honey. Why a stunning woman like you does not have a boyfriend?"

"And who exactly told you that I'm single?" she answered cheekily. The President loved the competition, and she knew it.

"I get it. I stole you from someone else," he caressed her cheek.

"Who knows," she added audaciously, giving him one of those looks with which she had so often impressed the jury. Her impertinence shook him "You know what? I like the competition, but you'll have to choose who you want to be with when the right time comes," he said to impress her.

Cecilia was just starting to relax. For some reason, in this place, so far from everything and everyone, it seemed that her secrets were easier to hide. They had dinner by the sea, with their feet in the sand. Fernando wanted to impress her; he was completely fascinated by the beauty of this woman. The typical South American, but with something more.

As for Cecilia she decided the time had come to ask him more personal questions; as usual, when you start dating someone. She tried to focus on the person, rather than on the position he held. This gave her the naturalness necessary to enchant him. They talked about their childhood and youth, their families and the obstinacy they had imposed on themselves in pursuing their goals.

"I always thought that with determination and hard work, life could have offered me more than the ordinary," he said.

"Ordinary is for ordinary people," she echoed. Then there was a long pause during which she ate the last prawn that remained on her plate, before asking an indiscreet question, "You didn't tell me something. Are you a bachelor?"

From under his big dark mustache Fernando curved his lips into a mysterious smile "What does it matter if I'm single, or not?"

"I get it!" she got angry "You're one of those typical man"

"-I am not typical at all, Cecilia. You'll find out," he said seriously.

After dinner, they strolled along the beach. The security service did not lose sight of them while following Rodriguez and the Miss discreetely discreetly from afar. Fernando took her hand and they walked together, bathing their feet in the water like two teenagers. For a moment, he forgot who he was, and time seemed to have gone back.

He had the feeling he'd known that woman since forever. Cecilia let herself be carried away by his enthusiasm. She discovered that, contrary to what she thought, Rodríguez had a strong sense of humor. They ended up dancing merengue, on the notes of a famous song that he began to hum, although he could not remember any single lyric. Eventually, they bathed naked and embraced in the warm water of the Caribbean Sea. It was she who had lifted her dress up to her knees to get into the sea. Fernando hadn't thought about it for a moment. He quickly got full undressed and followed her.

When he reached her, he took her in his arms, kissing her stubbornly. Using just one hand he undressed her, and threw her silk dress towards the sand. He went into ecstasy when her turgid nipples rubbed against his chest. He took off her panties. She let him do it, and kissed him intensely. Fernando's hands began to run down her chest, and then lingered on her hips, before exploring her more intimate parts. He looked her in the eyes for a moment, as if waiting to receive confirmation from her of the sensations that his movements brought her. She grabbed her shoulders and spread her legs astride. The rubbing of her vulva against his member produced an electric shock which culminated in an erection. "Touch me" she whispered, biting his ear wet with water and salt. Panting, Fernando surrounded her and pulled her towards him. His penis entered perfectly inside her, giving him a divine sensation. He put his hands around her pelvis and started to move. With the movement, Cecilia felt the water amplify her pleasure and her heart beat faster and stronger until, after a moment that she didn't know how to quantify, she exploded with pleasure.

Cecilia jumped out of the water, wringing her long hair in

her hands. Not bad at all! She said to herself, remembering how hot the men of his land were. Luckily she was on contraceptive pill. When on the shore, she was surprised to see that two large blue towels had magically appeared on the sand. She then looked around, but saw no one.

"Do not worry. The service is very discreet. They don't see and they don't say anything," said Fernando, who was right behind her. He kissed her on the shoulder before helping her get dry. "You didn't expect that, did you?" He bent to his knees to get the second towel.

"No. It was totally unexpected," she replied

"For me too," he echoed.

That night they fell asleep together in his bed. They chatted a bit, until he fell asleep. Cecilia was insomniac. Her mind, haunted with thoughts, swirled. She started thinking about Tom. What was he doing now? *What am I supposed to do?* If she had retrieved her bag in her room, she could have carried on the plan. The product that the CIA had given her so that she could administered it to Fernando was hidden in the inside pocket of her clutch bag. So she decided to try to get it. She moved slowly to the edge of the bed. Just when she was about to put her foot on the ground, Fernando turned snoring. Cecilia immediately froze and hoped she hadn't woken him up. As she clearly felt he turning in his sleep she thought *Fuck!*

She tiptoed towards the exit as she approached the door she noticed the shadows of the guards who patrolled the external corridor whose shadow was created by the light of the lamps of the patio. They were right outside their door. *I can't get out of here!* She freaked. She went to the bathroom where she rinsed her face under running cold water; then she drank some water and went back to bed. *I have to get in contact with Miranda, but how do I do it?* Without knowing what to do she began to pray to the virgin of Ávila to give her the strength she needed to move forward. Until, exhausted, she fell into a deep sleep, without even realizing it.

She suddenly opened her eyes and looked around her. She was alone. Little birds sang outside of the window. She stretched her neck and inspected the room. For a moment she hoped to be in her home. She had just dreamed about all of this. But with despair she noticed that the images her eyes were returning to her brain stated the opposite. *I am still here!*

She went to her room, where she got dressed, before going downstairs to the halls for breakfast. Milly waited for her with her welcoming smile "Good morning, Miss!"

"Good morning. Call me Cecilia, please" she put a hand on her shoulder.

"Did you sleep well?"

"Fantastic, thank you!"

"Come with me. The President is having breakfast by the swimming pool. "She walked quickly. They passed through various rooms that Cecilia had not yet seen. The palace was huge and very old. Cecilia approached the balustrade before going down the stairs. **Today I will have to administer that product to him, of course.**

Fernando was sitting under the shade of an umbrella. As always, he was talking on the phone. As soon as he saw her, his face lit up in a big smile. He invited her to sit down.

"The people must understand that I am the one who improved their existence! Without me the American enemy will take over. Is this what they want? Pure capitalism?" He frowned. "Listen, Hugo. You know it. The rich are evil. Absolute evil! I am the only good thing that has happened in this country since Simon Bolívar's time. So either they all close their mouths, or I will be forced to send them to the mines!" He closed the conversation theatrically, exhaling deeply.

"Good morning darling. Did you sleep well?"

"Very well, thank you. The bed was very comfortable indeed. What problems are there in the early morning?"

"It's just that people don't understand a damn thing!" He exploded "they don't understand that Venezuela is an independent country. A country rich in its own. They believe that Americans would solve their problems, but America is the problem!"

"My beautiful *papi*. I do not understand you. Explain these things to me!" Maybe it was a good opportunity to extract some more information from him.

"We are a very rich country. We produce more oil than the rest of Latin America, and do we want someone to suck our blood? I say no!" He was furious.

"Oh my love, don't get angry! But tell me, how come people are so poor if we are such a rich country? I do not understand"

"This is also the fault of the Americans! They want to kick me out and they started making a policy against me. An economic war, made of sanctions and embargo. But it's them who stopped buying our oil. It was them who generated the chronic devaluation of our currency. And we united as Venezuelans, will resist the foreign conqueror!"

Cecilia thought it was easy to talk like this when you own a private island. "But then why are there so many riots against you?"

"It is the Americans who pay people to make these protests. They always have an enemy to find, and this time it's me. They make me bad publicity, but all they say is nonsense!" He slammed his fist on the table.

Nonsense. For him, people who starved on the streets were nonsense; children raised in orphanages after their parents died killed in some *ranchos* fights were nonsense; that a pack of rice costed the equivalent of half an employee's monthly salary, was nonsense. Cecilia's blood began to boil in in her veins. She looked at her purse in which she had hidden the lethal product. The words of the CIA chief rang in her mind: the administration of a small amount of that powder will be enough to cause him deadly liver cancer in a few weeks. Nobody will suspect you, or us.

"Do you know that they tried to kill me several times? But I've always caught them," Fernando added triumphantly. Cecilia smiled forcefully as she felt her cheeks flare up. To keep him from noticing that, she said, "I admire you Fernando a lot. Your position isn't easy"

"It is not. But I am convinced of what I do, and the others will have nothing else to do but adapt." He closed the topic of the conversation.

"Now tell me. What would you like to do today?"

CHAPTER 14

Washington

Agent Mulligan hung up the phone. He took a deep breath and looked out of his office window. Spring had arrived there too. He got up and headed for the coffee machine next to the gray sofa in front of his desk. *So Mendoza is gone.* This wasn't good news. The only good news was that officially no one would trace her back to them if, for some reason, something had gone terribly wrong. They would have covered their asses without any problem. For this reason, it was good to use resources like Cecilia who was an outsider. Outsiders could not be classified as infiltrates, because they were not from the organization, and they could not play double agents as they had no contact in this world. They were the perfect solution. A solution that would have saved his ass. They were what they called in the jargon, the blind operators. Or as he and his colleagues would call them *the prostitutes*. The system was indeed the same. You collected them on the street, you paid them for their services and wave goodbye! They didn't know anything about you, and you didn't know anything about them. You went home quietly, without anyone suspecting about anything. This was Cecilia: a prostitute who had left him manipulate her. It had been easy with her. It was always easy with prostitutes. They couldn't even begin to suspect the intricacy behind the situations in which they got involved. Convincing them was easy. Indeed, it is assumed that in the collective imagination the United States are always the good ones. "The city up on a hill" at the core of the American exceptionalism. It didn't matter where you lived, the American system had without any reasonable doubt penetrated into your brain through television, cinema, music. It had shaped you in such a way that you really believed all the things they wanted you to believe in. With outsiders it was that easy. Let them watch some bad news about your enemy, and they bought it. They would fall for it leading you to win your battle. *A piece of cake* thought Mulligan before returning to his desk. Yet there was a problem that he had to solve immediately. *Where's Mendoza?* Only one person had the answer to this question.

CHAPTER 15

Paradise Island

The Caribbean Sea gently caressed her legs that hung sideways from the deckchair on which she'd been relaxing for hours. Every time the water reached the shore the legs of the deckchair got wet. She had missed this sea. Her sea. Cecilia turned her head and looked at the escort, who did not lose sight of her for a minute. She was supposed to call Miranda, but how? In reality there was no way. Her phone was intercepted; they would have discovered her plan right away, and if she had gone to the city center with an excuse, the escort would have accompanied her. How could she justify to make a phone call from a public phone when she had a cell phone in her pocket? She wasn't even sure she would find a public phone. So nothing, she had to figure it out on her own, as usual.

Agent Perez was sitting under a palm tree. A few meters from him, a large iguana ate the remains of his sandwich; the ones he'd thrown at the iguana earlier. The beauty queen had been laid on that deckchair since the morning, and it was up to him to make sure that nothing happened to her.

What the hell shall be happen to her anyway?

The heat and humidity were unbearable on that day, in which not even a gust of wind blew. Suddenly, the voice of the President's assistant interrupted his thoughts through the Walkie Talkie. "The President has finished his meetings. Please bring Ms. Mendoza here."

"Got it," he said. He glanced at his colleague who was standing and looking at him "Time to move. Call her."

An hour later Cecilia was lying in bed next to Fernando. They had sex twice in a row and finally relaxed next to each other. Cecilia adjusted her chestnut coloured hair on the pillow and, for a moment, let herself be lulled by the feeling of well-being that the orgasm had caused her. She had to recognize that even if he never believed it possible, this man knew how to make love.

Even if she was struggling to admit it, even to herself, there was something about him that she liked. Yes, he was rude and very presumptuous but, nevertheless he was also young, handsome, determined and intelligent, plus he had something else that made him even more fascinating in Cecilia's eyes: power.

"I feel comfortable with you," Fernando said, grabbing a lock of her beautiful hair between his fingers. Cecilia didn't know what to say "Tell me how long will you be keeping me here, indefinitely segregated?" She joked. Fernando understood from this apparently innocent claim that she wanted to know more about how long their stay would have lasted. And he was not ready to divulge this information just yet. In fact, he wanted to give her no certainty. He was like that. He enjoyed the feeling of power when keeping people in the dark of his intentions.

"Don't you like being here with me, *mi reina*?"

"Of course I like it. But what do we do? Are we staying here indefinitely?"

"And even if it was the case, would it bother you? Cecilia didn't understand if it was a joke

"No, but I guess I'll have to get back to work sooner or later," she protested.

"What if I told you that from now on, you don't have to

work one day in your life again?"

Cecilia's eyes widened "You like being enigmatic, don't you?"

"Yes and you like me to be"

"And won't you tell me how long we will stay here?"

"Who cares?"

"Me?"

"I'll tell you a secret. We will stay here until you fall in love with me"

"Come on, stop joking!" The girl protested

"Soon you will discover something about me: I never ever joke" He got out of bed and dressed up.

"I have a meeting. See you later." He leaned over to kiss her on the shoulder in the same way he did the day before, and then left. Cecilia no longer knew what to do. Everything seemed strange to her, she didn't feel comfortable. It occurred to her that perhaps they had uncovered her mission and that for this reason he'd brought her to the island.

The President not only had informants, but he was a smart guy; he certainly was! But it didn't make sense. Nothing made sense. Why sleep with her if he suspected her to be an infiltrate? As always, many questions that vanished like drops in the rain, without answers.

A few hours later, Cecilia put her foot in the water while she waited for Fernando to arrive. She got up from the table and walked to the shore. The water was warm. She glanced at the display of her phone which marked 20.17 minutes.

"Sorry, honey. The meeting was longer than expected. I'm here now!" Fernando said approaching her in his linen trousers with a blue jacket.

"You got dressed up *papi*," she said sitting down at the table.

"Of course! I'll do everything to make my *reina* happy," he said, sitting on the straw chair too. The waiters served empanadas and carne mechada traditional recipes that Cecilia's mother used to prepare when they were kids. It was two of her favorite dishes.

"Delicious! I love carne mechada and empanadas. What a coincidence!" she smiled. For tonight Cecilia wouldn't even bother with her diet. Fernando laughed from under his mustache "They cooked this especially for you. There's no coincidence here, honey," he said.

"I can not believe it!"

"And still you have seen nothing," he shook her hand on the table.

Mariachis emerged out of nowhere and started playing classic Venezuelan songs, such as Simon Diaz's Caballo Viejo. The Two remained chatting amiably for a time that seemed to both very short. The waiters served more and more food. Everything was delicious. Cecilia now seemed relaxed. Her eyes darted in the direction of Fernando. The electricity between the two was evident, it had filled the air. Suddenly she looked at him gently for a moment, before diverting her big brown eyes towards the plate in front of her. This was the look Fernando was waiting for. A look that said it all. *This is the moment* he thought. When the delicious passion fruit sorbet was served, Cecilia dared to ask "I still don't understand which island we are on?"

"It's called Paradise Island," he said, savoring the home-made sorbet.

"But there is no island called paradise" she remembered from her geography classes.

"You're right, before it was called Isla Margarita. Now that it is mine I have decided to change its name. Margherita made no sense even though, historically, it was called that way because in Greek *Margheritis* are pearls and here there are many pearls. But I didn't like it. So I changed it. You do not like it?"

"I love it!"

"I am delighted"

"And the name Venezuela, do you like it?" She chuckled

"Sure! It's the name of our nation!"

"Doesn't the origin of that name bother you?" She challenged him and caught him off guard. A calculated move.

"And what would its origin be? Miss *I know everything*?" He taunted her.

She adjusted her figure into the chair "You know. When Christopher Columbus first arrived on our coasts, he entered the delta of the Orinoco River" she made a pause, examining Fernando's reaction to the word Orinoco. His expression did not change slightly and therefore she proceeded telling

"When seeing the stilts on the water, Columbus who was Italian, had the impression that he was in Venice and so called this place *Veneziola* which means Little Venice in Italian, from that the name Venezuela comes!" she said proud of having remembered this detail of when she had studied history of Venezuela in school.

"I see you know your subjects" he did not mention that he never knew this story as he'd never attended school "So let's see. It might be an idea to change it into something more nationalist. A name that is far away from those colonial times, that came after the discovery" he added.

"Let me get this straight If you don't like something, you just change it?" she teased him.

"Of course! It's what I've always done, and what I'll always do."

"What other things don't you like?"

"I don't like injustice. I don't like that others decide for our country. That people make decisions based on the economy without seeing what people want. I don't like this," he paused masterfully. Cecilia thought that he had a fixation on this matter.

"Now ask me what I like" Cecilia smiled for this was a very stupid game. "I really mean it. Ask me," he insisted.

"All right. What do you like?"

"You" he let that one word echoed in Cecilia's mind, before continuing. "I like you very much and that's why I have something for you" he made a gesture with his hand towards the back, and lingered in amusement over her astonished expression. Cecilia's heart skipped a beat for a moment. *What other surprise did this man have for me now!?*

Rodríguez's assistant approached the table with a velvet box in his hand.

"Cecilia Mendoza I am a determined man who knows exactly what he wants, and I made my decision. Will you marry me?" He opened the box revealing a huge 10-carat pure diamond. Cecilia put a hand on her chest. She definitely couldn't believe it!

"Fernando!? Are you joking!?"

He waited a moment before answering her, high on his own vanity. Afterall he has this temper.

"Like I said, I never joke. Marry me." He said as if it was an order.

"But we've known each other for so little ..." she gasped

"I know. But believe me: you don't get where I am in life if you don't have clear ideas. From the first moment I saw you, I thought you would become my wife. This is why *I waited a long time* to ask you. I wanted to be sure you wanted it too."

Cecilia made an effort to keep her mouth closed. *Had he waited so long? It hadn't been even a week since they'd met!?*

"I am sorry. How do you know I want it !?"

"I just happen to know. So far I didn't know, and you didn't know either. But tonight, I noticed something in your gaze that has changed, and therefore I decided that the moment had come" in that instant he felt like a number one. Cecilia asked the question to herself. Had he really noticed that she was falling in love with him? Wow! Life was a roll coaster! She had gone there to poison this man, and now she had fallen in love with him.

"But Fernando... what are you babbling about!? When did you understand that I had fallen in love with you? And how did you do that?" She begged for an explanation. This time Fernando decided to supply the information to her without hesitation.

"Right then, when you gave me that look, a moment after the sorbet was served. It was there when you fell in love with me. I could clearly sense it"

In fact there had been a specific moment in which Cecilia had felt different. As if something inside her had clicked. A feeling she had never experienced before in her life.

"So, Miss Mendoza. For how long are you considering to leave your President on hold?" Fernando was sure she wouldn't say no. He could just read it inside of her.

"Sorry it's ... this is ... so ... unbelievable!" Her voice was struggling to get out of her mouth.

"Say yes. And then you will discover new meanings to attribute to the word *unbelievable*"

"But you understand, I don't know anything about you!"

"You will it find out step by step. I'll tell you something." He took her by the hand, setting his eyes inside hers. "You and I are the same. We come from misery and we managed to get to the top. We are two of a kind. We have achieved our goals and moved forward. We are proud, bastards and extremely concrete. We don't let ourselves be influenced by what others say, and this is our best quality. We are smart and vultures, courageous and responsible. We are ambitious and determined. Nobody can stop us, because we simply are the best. Do you know how many people there are like us in this world? About 1% of the population. Do you know why? Because everyone tries to be like us, but only we have managed to succeed in becoming what we wanted to be"

Those words left Cecilia astonished. It was as if he had known her forever, as if he had read inside of her, in her deepest thoughts. As if he had access to her soul. For the first time in her life, the mask of fighter she would put on began to crumble. She stayed there like a sitting duck. A naked girl in front of her fragilities. All of her certainties were swept away in a snap and she decided to answer the only thing that she really wanted to "Yes. I want to marry you!" She shouted excitedly as Fernando put the huge pear-shaped brilliant on her finger. They kissed frantically.

"Well! I love you!" Fernando hugged her. He called his assistant who had left after passing over the ring to him.

"Jorge! Come here! The young lady said yes then let's not waste time: we get married tomorrow in the basilica of *Nuestra Señora de El Valle*! Prepare everything."

"Very well Mr. President and congratulations to you and the young lady!"

A bottle of expensive French champagne appeared under their noses, in a flash. Cecilia still hadn't had time to metabolise what had just happened.

"To health, my love, and to our happiness!" Fernando omitted the words love, money and sex because he already had them.

"To you, Fernando!"

I need to find a phone ASAP!

At three in the afternoon of the following day, Cecilia Mendoza, Miss Universe 2014, made her triumphal entry into the basilica of Our Lady of the Valley. The church in pure colonial style was made even more spectacular by the sublime floral decorations that adorned both the interior and the exterior. The square had been closed for the event. People were gathering behind the barriers the mayor had placed.

When the Rolls Royce pulled up in front of the church, Cecilia's heart pounded and as she squeezed Milly's hand. "Don't worry honey! It is normal to be anxious in these moments. You are beautiful. Do not think about anything. Just have fun!" The old lady suggested.

Cecilia simply nodded and blew the air out of her lungs. Dr. Fliss' pills didn't seem to work today. She looked at Milly and was grateful that she was there to hold her hand. For a minute it seemed to her that her mother was in her place in that car.

"Take it easy. Everything will be fine." Milly went back to thinking that Cecilia was just undergoing the typical emotion of all the brides in the world. But it wasn't just that. It was anxiety mixed with fear. *What if they'd discovered that I am already married?* She wondered.

In a few moments she would have received the first answer to the 1000 questions that floated in her head since the beginning of this charade.

"Ready when you want, and congratulations," said the driver. A man in a uniform approached the car door and opened it. It was he who would walk the bride to the altar

"Congratulations," he said, stretching out his arm so that she could lean on it.

"Here we are. Come on," said Cecilia. They slowly entered the packed church. The wonderful wedding dress she wore had arrived that morning from Miami together with a dressmaker from the atelier of the *Maison* who had the task of retouching it so that it adhered perfectly to her beautiful figure. Next to the altar, Fernando was in his most elegant uniform. He wore the sash and collar of the Order of the Libertador.

For a moment Cecilia thought that he looked like one of those princes she had seen in Montecarlo at the galas. She approached with a smile as the notes of the wedding march echoed in the air. If someone had told her, only five years earlier, that in life she would had achieved all this, she would have laughed out loud.

A few steps away surrounded by his loyalists, Fernando kept smiling down at her. There were people sitting in the front row and Cecilia thought they were certainly the Rodríguez's, whom, obviously, she had not yet been introduced.

As required, the men who walked her down the aisle lifted her veil up before handle the bride to the President and sat down on the side of the bride's witnesses. It is curious that Cecilia didn't even know who her witnesses was. She marveled herself by looking at those people on her left side in their tight uniforms.

"You are beautiful!" Fernando whispered in her ear "I'm the happiest and luckiest man in the world" she felt her cheeks turn red and dampen a chuckle into the bouquet of white orchids she was holding in her hands. The orchid is the symbol of Venezuela, and the bouquet was matching her beautiful Cartier orchid shaped diamond earrings the President had given her that morning.

To her surprise, the mass was celebrated without any trouble. Nobody noticed that she was already married. *The* CIA *had done its job very well*, she thought while signing the register at the end of the liturgy.

"Long live the President and the First Lady!" the Generals exclaimed in chorus together with the high dignitaries of the State. The bride and groom came out of the church under a row of swords that the military had risen above their heads and then posed for the usual wedding portraits.

"Are you happy, my love?"

"Immensely"

"You are now the First Lady of Venezuela," he smiled.

"Just three days ago I would never had imagined it"

They left the church under the sun of the eternal Caribbean summer, towards what it would have been the most beautiful day of their lives.

Two hours later, Cecilia had changed into a short white dress. The make-up artist and hairdresser were busy fixing her hair and make-up. For a moment it seemed to her that she was back to the Miss Universe contest. As always, she had given them instructions about how her hair should have looked big and voluminous. More and more voluminous. This time the hairdresser had not dared to say anything. After all, who could protest before the First Lady's pretensions?

The wedding banquet lasted until dawn. French champagne and caviar and giant lobsters were served. The mariachis played the songs of their youth, while one hundred guests, mostly big fish from the Government, paid their respects to the newly wed. Fernando was happy. After the hustle and bustle of his first mariage, he was resigned he would never meet someone who made him feel like this again. Just when he had given up hope, fate had made him meet Cecilia, a beautiful but courageous woman, just like him.

His men had been formidable. They had organized everything in just eight hours. The whole country had been mobilized. State planes had brought guests, decorations, food and chefs from all regions back and forth in order to organize their wedding party.

"Do whatever she tells you," Rodríguez had said to his assistant in charge of orchestrating everything. That was a dream wedding party.

After dinner, the bride and groom opened the dances tied in a waltz.

"I wish this night would last forever" he whispered in her

ear, leaving Cecilia speechless. Fernando was a romantic when he wanted to.

After the first waltz was over, Fernando called his loyalists and invited General Aguirre to replace him. To dance with his wife.

"Sorry Cecilia, I have to speak with the Ministers. I'll leave you in good hands," he said

"Aguirre! Be careful of my lady. I'm watching you!" He joked

"Do not worry. I will treat her like a delicate flower," he replied, receiving the message.

"Good. That's fine. I trust you" Fernando disappeared inside of the house. All the eyes of the guests were now focused on the bride and Aguirre.

"Congratulations Ms. Rodríguez," he said to break the ice.

"Thank you General"

"Who could have foreseen all this happening just a few days ago?" He looked around him at the thousand lights that decorated the transparent marquee.

"Life is incredible," she sighed, trying not to get too close to him.

"Will you allow me a dance?" General Miranda's voice echoed behind them.

"Of course, Miranda. But handle her with care: this woman it's a delicate flower"

"All exotic flowers look delicate, Aguirre." He replied "But they aren't really. They are strong and brave, to resist tropical storms and hurricanes. So don't worry, I'll take care of her. Mrs. Rodríguez, may I?" he held out his hand.

Cecilia looked down without knowing what to say.

"What a surprise to see you here, General," she said as he girded her waist.

"True, huh? Imagine how many surprises I've received in the past three days," he made her turn under his arm.

"It was a sudden unexpected event," she justified herself.

"Obviously. And you love those unexpected surprises, don't you? Especially when they bring money and power," he twirled her again under his arm.

"What did the others say?"

"Oh! Mrs. Rodríguez, here comes the fun part. Everyone wonders why you disappeared, where you'd been and they are all convinced that you have sold yourself to the highest bidder. I can't wait to see Mulligan's face when he knows what's going on here tonight" another spin.

Cecilia remained silent letting him speak. "Aren't they going to be angry?" She asked.

The General started laughing "Angry? Your choice of words is interesting. They are not angry .... they are furious!!"

"But what was I supposed to do?"

Miranda was clenching her hands firmly now. "What was expected for you to do from the first moment, and not for you to get carried away on a vacation while people are starving. I knew we couldn't trust someone like you! A beauty queen! Ah! How silly!!"

"I don't see what the problem is. I chose to be a Miss in my life and that's what I managed to do so well!" now Cecilia deserved some respect.

"Sure! You did it. But you managed to get to the top only by relying on compromise! Which is how people like you move forward in life"

Cecilia was offended "careful General. For now, it takes me a second to explain to my husband who you really are!"

"Sure. And tell me, because the question intrigues me: what husband would you explain who I am. This husband or the other one?"

"Enough!" Cecilia kept pretending to laugh as if the General was telling her something funny. But she was meanwhile trying to discreetly push him away.

"Where are you going Cecilia?" he whispered in her ear as she was pulling her hand away from his. "Everyone is staring at us. So I suggest you keep on smiling. Come on, like this, good girl ... let them think we are having lots of fun"

"Leave me alone!" she said when the song finished and finally she was able to freed herself. Miranda grabbed her hand and pretended to be kissing it. "Be careful, Cecilia. We have all the material on you. If Rodrìguez knows who you really are, he will kill you like a dog; and believe me, he won't hesitate for a second. I advise you to hurry up to do what you have to do. It will be better for everyone. You have a week to do it, after that we come looking for you" and just then he let her hand go.

Suddenly Cecilia realized what she had done, the mess she was stacked in.

With a smile her new husband returned to the dance floor where he exclaimed "I have to thank you Miranda. If it wasn't for you I would never have known my wife! I'll have to reward you for the favour." Miranda had to disguise his disgust. "Thank you Mr. President, it's an honour for me. Don't worry the fact that you invited me to your wedding ceremony is already a gift for me."

"I insist. I need a new Director for the national oil company. You know... the old manager didn't do well" he put a hand on his shoulder. Miranda knew that the old Director had been defenestrated and imprisoned on charges of being anti-governmental and pro-American.

"Come on. Come with me. Let's go inside to talk about your future"

"Now? Miranda asked. Given the circumstance, it did not seem the most appropriate moment. "Don't wait for tomorrow to do what you can do today. Let's go to my office now" and they walked.

Miranda sat down on the armchair on the other side of the President's desk. He ordered the same drink as Rodríguez's to the waiter who diligently asked the question. The President cleared his throat. "Your chance to cover yourself with glory and money is here." Miranda inspected Rodríguez's black eyes.

"Thank you Mr. President, but I know nothing about oil"

"You don't need to know these things. There is a team that deals with the practical aspects. The important thing is that you are in charge of the largest company in this country. After all, the people's money comes from there." Miranda was used to these slogan phrases that the President used frequently during his long speeches to the nation. Generally, he spoke of the people being oppressed by the foreign enemy, but never concluding anything concrete. People continued to starve, mortality in the country had increased by five times.

"Excuse me Mr. President, but I think for this same reason my contribution to the people would be quite useless in that particular function."

Rodríguez frowned and relaxed in the armchair, touching his chin with his fingers.

"Are you saying no, General?"

"I don't say that! But I think we should make sure we have expert people to work for Venezuela's first company. Someone with experience, so that our enemies cannot exploit our inexperience to damage us."

"I do not trust anybody. Only my Generals. If Venezuela is doing so badly, it is because wealthy capitalists have taken advantage of the system for years! And with the complicity of the Government! Banco Latino fell apart when American capitalists tried to steal our money by depreciating the Bolívar. Do you remember, General? I can't let this happen again, so tell me how much you want to run the oil company and let's move on!"

Miranda had tried, but he knew that resisting or even worse, not accepting the assignment would have probably made him imprisoned on the charge of being a traitor of the country. Then he took the pen in front of him and wrote, on a piece of paper, a figure that seemed adequate for the assignment. The President's eyes analyzed every movement he made. When he finished he placed the piece of paper under Rodríguez's watchful eyes.

"Well. We have a deal! Tomorrow it will be your fists day".

Miranda thanked him by shaking his hand. He strove to tell a joke, so that the President didn't suspect anything. Together, in a friendly and relaxed atmosphere, they returned to the huge transparent marquee where the guests continued to dance.

Now what shall I do? He wondered, emptying down a glass of port. *How will I be able to explain this to Mulligan?*

CHAPTER 16

Washington

The next day at seven sharp in the morning Carter, as always, was swimming in his magnificent Olympic-size pool which he builded in the veranda. Fatigue started to kick in. *Only have five left*, he thought, mentally counting down how many laps were left to reach 100. The final part was always the most difficult, but it was only in harsh times when you could see what a man was made of. *Resilience*. In the silence of the morning, his phone's buzzing sounded particularly loud.

Carter was surprised. *Who would break my balls so early?* He thought it must be urgent and went straight to the ladder. If they had called just five minutes later, he would have completed his training. This is how you lose a war. When alien circumstances stand between you and your goal. He shook his hair up before walking towards his cell phone which was on the table next to one of the deck chairs. When his wife had bought it, he thought they were ugly and expensive. Now, after seeing them every day for the past fifteen years, he thought they were only expensive.

"Carter" replied closing his watch around his wrist.

"Mulligan," his voice said it all. Something went wrong, very wrong.

"What happened?" he said focusing on the call

"We are in shit. A lot of shit."

CHAPTER 17

Paradise Island

Cecilia woke up in her new home. For a moment, she thought once again, that all of that had happened in her dreams. The engagement ring and the pristine wedding band that shone on her finger brought her back to reality. It had really happened! She couldn't refrain from smiling while looking around. There was nothing this girl from *Coche* couldn't achieve!

In that precise moment Milly entered.

"Good morning Madame. Everything is ready for your honeymoon. Do you want to check what I packed for you?" She made sure.

"Honeymoon?" Cecilia rubbed her eyes. She knew nothing about a honeymoon. And where were they supposed to be off to?

"Yes Madame. The yacht is anchored right in front of the pier," she said as if it were the most normal thing in the world.

"The yacht ...?" She said in disbelief.

"Of course Madame, the President's yacht" she explained.

"Oh, don't worry Milly. I trust you when it comes to packing". She stood up quickly and dismissed the housekeeper.

A few hours later the sea water splashed on her face. She glanced at Fernando who, sitting next to her, was holding her hand. The tender took them to the boat sliding gently on the crystal clear waters of the Caribbean.

"Are you happy my love?" Fernando kissed her on the shoulder.

"*Si mi amor*" she replied "Who's yacht is this?" she naively asked while holding firmly between her fingers onto the brim of her hat so that the wind wouldn't carry it away.

"Take a guess?" he loved to see the expression on her face every time he surprised her. To mould people's feelings gave him a sensation of power.

"I didn't know you owned such a big boat!" she wowed. Her eyes were wide open "Let me rephrase: you didn't know *we* owned such a big boat".

"Let me rephrase: you didn't know we owned such a big boat." He corrected her. "You know nobody knows anything about me; all you read in the press is nothing but garbage. Look. I have another surprise for you," he said excitedly. As soon as the tender reduced its speed to approach the boat, the name of the vessel appeared before their eyes in huge capital letters.

BEAUTY QUEEN.

"Look it's for you!" He said proudly

"How did you do this? she covered her mouth with both hands in amazement.

"I simply ordered them to change the name of the boat yesterday. Because I wanted it to be dedicated to you," he shrugged.

Cecilia didn't even know if a boat's name could be changed so easily. Then she thought that her husband was the President and that whatever he desired the other ones shall obey. "Good morning President and First Lady" the Captain received them while other crew members helped them get on board.

"I am the captain and I am at your complete disposal to

make sure you'll have a wonderful stay" He introduced the staff members to her, while an attendant offered them refreshing wipes and delicious watermelon juice.

"She is Linda who is in charge of cleaning the cabins, then there is the plumber, the navigation assistant, the sailors, the three hubs ..." Cecilia was surprised to see how many people worked on that boat. Fernando, meanwhile, had gone to sit on the large oval sofa in the living room, and cooled down under the jet of the air conditioning. He liked to surprise her. There was something he adored in the fact that she always tried to resist him, but then she got carried away. As if she were a horse to be tamed. The horse is too proud to be tamed in an aggressive way. You'll have to conquer him until he trusts you. That was Cecilia, and so he had managed to conquer her.

The yacht warmed up the engines and began sailing in the Caribbean Sea towards Santa Lucia and the Grenadines.

Fernando himself wanted to show all the rooms on the four decks of the yacht to his wife. The large halls decorated in Italian style, the dining room that hosted up to twenty people and its large crystal table resting on stone sea horses. The elegant marble bathrooms with bathtub, the malachite fireplace to make love in front of it; a cinema with a popcorn machine; the gym full of equipment, the sauna and the Turkish bath; in addition to the outdoor swimming pool whose glass bottom was the roof of the disco.

"So while you dance you can see the stars," he explained. He showed her the helipad and the jet skis; and the bedrooms that looked like those of the Hermitage hotel in Montecarlo.

"It feels like being in an architecture magazine," she was thrilled as they entered the master bedroom. Fernando approached her from behind, holding her from the waist. He started kissing her behind the ear.

"Have you ever had sex on a yacht?" he asked, and without waiting for an answer he lifted her gently and put her down on the bed.

CHAPTER 18

The White House

Carter's hands were sweating. Trying not to show it, he rubbed them on his expensive custom-made *Caraceni* suit. The color was anthracite "and not dark gray" as the Italian tailor had corrected him. It was not his first time in the Oval Office, but it was the first time he had come with bad news. The first time something had gone wrong. President Truman, seated in front of him, was carefully reading about the developments of the top secret dossier he had brought to him. Codename: Orinoco.

Truman took a deep breath from his nostrils before taking off his glasses.

"Tell me Carter. How is it possible that the largest espionage agency in the world is not able to eliminate this problem? What am I supposed to think? That you are incompetent. Or that you do it on purpose?" Carter swallowed.

"Sir. We tried everything! We infiltrated agents. We made drone attacks. We financed drug trafficking as well as the opposition. We have corrupted half of South America, and lead the economy of the whole country to the brink of collapse. We have suspended the commercial agreements and lost huge contracts, and yet nothing has brought Rodríguez down" he justified himself. "But I have good news for you," he immediately added.

"And would it be?" Truman's little eyes peered at him.

"Our trusted man has been appointed Director of the Venezuelan oil company," he said down the hatch.

"Really? And it didn't occur to you that this person could be double gaming, shall we say?"

"Absolutely. He's one of ours, and no one else's. We have him in our pocket." He said.

"It seems to me that lately, things tend to slip out of your pocket quite easily"

Carter didn't know what to answer.

"Who came up with this idea of a Miss?" he asked provocatively.

"I did. I thought she was the perfect mole given Rodríguez's weakness for the fairer sex," he explained.

"And how did you think she could be trusted?" Carter didn't seem at all impressed by that inquisitive tone

"By blackmailing her. It's the only thing that works with woman like that. Blackmail."

"So you're telling me that you know her well, I deduce? In fact, I see how well you know her. So well that till now she hasn't done anything she was told, and she even married Rodríguez and ripped us off. A brilliant idea!"

"Blind operators have always worked in the past." He justified himself

"The fact that it worked in other circumstances does not automatically make it a good idea. If you have been lucky in the past, this does not mean that luck does not turn; exactly like the wind". Truman liked boats.

"But the reports and tests indicated that she was the perfect candidate-"

"-I don't care about reports and tests!" He silenced him. "My ass is at stake on this issue! And you have put my ass in the hands of a Miss! Did I make myself clear?" He pressed his finger down on the table to install more fear than what Carter already felt. "Now I demand that you move your ass, and quickly find an effective solution to the mess you've caused, do you understand me!?" Carter nodded.

"Very well. You have a week to close the Orinoco case, otherwise you can wave goodbye to your career and your six figure salary!" He threatened him

Carter emerged out from the meeting and exited discretely from the back door, the same one he'd entered. The driver brought his black car closer as soon as he saw him coming out from the door.

"Straight to your office, sir?" He asked.

"Yes please," he replied, loosening the knot on his tie. He took a bottle of water and took a big sip. Then he relaxed his shoulders on the comfortable seat. He noticed that his hands were no longer sweating. Now they were shaking.

Once alone in the oval room, Truman looked out of the window. *Time is put out*, he thought running a hand through his auburn hair. The elections would have been within a few months. 6 to be precise, and without the support of the Oil Association, his whole plan would have gone down the toilet. This was the deal: they would have guaranteed him a second mandate as long as he had unlocked the situation in Venezuela. Since that bastard of Rodríguez had arrived, foreign companies who had great interests in the Venezuelan oil had been expelled. Venezuela's immense oil wealth had been nationalized and extraction had plummeted. A maneuver orchestrated by Rodríguez which notwithstanding be very bold, had guaranteed Venezuela complete independence from abroad. The Oil Association, that was now hit by the economical turmoil's, needed to have access to that immense fortune. It was pivotal for reviving the American economy, create millions of jobs, and ensuring control of one of the geo-politically and strategically most important countries in the world: Venezuela. The certainties he had, now begun to crumble. For the first time, it was no longer sure of the only thing he had always taken for granted: his re-election. He inhaled and exhaled deeply, dwelling on Carter's words: Our trusted man has been appointed Director of the Venezuelan oil company, it could have been good news? Yes either no, depending on whether the newcomer would find the secret documents, or not.

He lifted the handset of the encrypted line and dialed the alphanumeric code corresponding to the number he wanted to contact. The person answered immediately.

"It's me. I need a favor," he said, stretching his legs on the table. He didn't speak much but what he said was clear and precise. Once the conversation was over, he adjusted the knot of his tie, looking at himself in one of the two mirrors on the side of his desk. He would not leave his fate in the hands of a band of incompetents. The next four years were to be the conclusion of his master's plan, according to which he would go down in history as the best President the United States ever had.

CHAPTER 19

La Campiña

Sitting in his new office in La Campiña, Miranda looked out the window. From the top floor of that tower you could see all of Caracas, and also the *ranchos* scattered on the peaks of the mountains. At night the dimmed lights made look the slum as a sort of nativity. But in the daylight all those display of disharmony shackes reminded of Dantes' inferno. And when rainy season and tropical thunderstorms kicked in the ranchos would be dragged down onto the valley in a mash of mud and metal sheets. That was the time in which the center of hell had been reached.

A pair of splendid yellow-blue macaws flew before his eyes. *God knows why they always fly in pairs. How do they endure for so many years together?* He wondered knowing that the average life for those animals was close to one hundred years. From a distance he also saw a *zamuro,* or a vulture flying high, perhaps in search of a prey or a carcass to feast on.

"Miss, would you please bring me all the documentation?" he asked to his secretary over the intercom. If he was to run this business, he had to know everything there was to know.

"I'll be right in, Director," Sara said who ten minutes later appeared in his doorway. Her platinum dyed blonde hair as if she was Swedish did not quite matched her creole skin color. She entered the door dragging a heavy cart. Instinctively Miranda got up to help her.

"My God! How many papers!" he exclaimed pulling the

cart.

"I know. Your predecessor was not a big fan of technology. He preferred paper and so he filled the archives with documents that could have been easily stored online. He just didn't want to" she explained

"Okay, thanks, you can go now" he got rid of her and started immediately digging into the papers.

Miranda spent the day reading a pile of documents about the company's history, the work that had been done, the medium and long-term objectives, the statistics and the annual reports. Even if he wasn't a specialist on the matter he could tell that something was wrong. Although couldn't figure out what.

Why had a company that could produce millions of barrels a day, cut production like this overnight? It made no sense from any side you were looking at it.

Outside, the black sky signaled that the night had come. Time for him to go home where his wife Francisca was waiting for him.

CHAPTER 20

Saint Lucia

The peaks of the two most famous mountains of Santa Lucia were only at a distance of a good swim. Letting herself be lulled by the fluctuations of the boat, Cecilia was sitting on the stern with her husband who had just returned on board after a swim.

La dolce vita

"It's full of fish down here, you should see them, they are beautiful"

"Can I ask you something?" Cecilia changed posture.

"Sure," he said, passing a towel over his hairy chest.

"Why are things so bad in Venezuela? What do we need to be a rich country?" Her husband frowned. Where did this question come from for the second time?

"It's that I really don't understand it. Such a beautiful country ... and it's bankrupt, why?"

Fernando sat next to her feeling his wife's frustration. "As a young man I also asked myself the very same question every day. Only years later, I got my answers. If I tell you the truth, you would be very surprised." He glanced down at her eyes who were looking for an explanation at all costs.

"I could tell you that it is the fault of one or the others. But the truth is, we are all guilty in this game. All of us. Guilty of accepting this system. See Cecilia, we were once slaves to the colonizers, and we continue to be slaves. The world does not change, and the wealth of some is built on the shoulders of others"

For the first time, Cecilia sensed that he had put aside the constant effort of trying to impress her, and that he was telling her the truth.

"I do not understand?"

"The world is not fair. It has never been, and never will be. Never. Despite the efforts, that's how the system works," he said resignedly.

A slight breeze began to blow. Fernando took advantage of the sublime view that was his wife in her white skimpy bikini that left little to the imagination.

"Come on let's go to the sun before you'll get cold."

Three days later the presidential helicopter brought them back to reality. Exactly a week had passed, since she was still only a Miss who had accepted his invitation, and now, in such a short time, she had become the First Lady of her country. Had she passed on the other side of the barricade, or not?

The residence of La Casona looked like a flower shop, for the many bouquets that she had received from all those who congratulated her on the wedding.

The assistants did nothing but bomb her with questions. How did she wanted to renovate the rooms? Did she wanted to change something? While her husband's counsellors explained to her the proper protocol and etiquette that should have been put in place during presidential events, it was immediately apparent that her brain was struggling to grind that amount of information. Everyone thought it must be normal to give her some time to settle into her new life. But in reality Cecilia could think of nothing but Miranda's words. The fateful date was only three days away.

"Sorry, we'll see this later. Now I'm not feeling well," she lied, feeding the rumours that were spreading along the staff that she was already pregnant. Which would also explain the reason for such a sudden marriage. She went up to her new room, very similar in style to the halls below. She admired the white walls and the wooden ceilings, while the thoughts in her head swirled. Was she really sure she wanted to do this? And above all, was this really helpful to her people? She went through all the elements. Her mother hiding somewhere in the middle of nowhere in the United States with her sister. Tom, jailed God knows where. Miranda who probably had already told everything to everyone. Agent Mulligan who had certainly taken precautions to warn his superiors. What could she do now? She didn't know, but she had to do it as soon as possible. The longer she waited, the more suspicious they would be. So she called Miranda.

"Good evening, General," she said with a big smile on her face

"First Lady! What an honor to receive your call." He was very surprised.

"I have received your flowers. They are splendid!"

"I hope you like them," he said even though he hadn't sent her any flowers.

"I'd like to see you, to thank you. I wouldn't have found the man of my life if it wasn't for you General"

"Don't worry," Miranda played along knowing that the conversations were intercepted.

"My husband and I insist that you come over to dinner tonight. We look forward to seeing you" and that's how she ended the call.

A shiver of cold ran over the General's shoulders. He no longer knew what game she played, but one thing was certain: he couldn't decline the invitation.

Three hours later the car arrived in La Casona, where he was informed that the First Lady was waiting for him in the gardens. *She is not stupid for a Miss*, he told himself as he headed towards the only place where bugs could hardly have recorded anything: the gardens. He met her in the area of tropical plants, dressed all in white while arranging freshly cut flowers, in a vase. She greeted him as one would greet an old friend. She hugged him and showed him the wonderful engagement ring, inviting him to take a stroll. Miranda took her by the arm, as was normal for a gentleman of his age to do.

"There is little time left..." he said, leaving the sentence in mid-air.

"I know, but I don't know what to do"

"Of course you do"

"I'm not sure. I mean, what if it's all a big lie?"

"It's not your role to ask questions, you just have to perform."

"What if I don't?"

"Then you can say *hasta la vista* to your husband, to the money, to everything and everyone"

"Are we really sure that the situation will be really better afterwards?" The General was not used to doubts arising. All his life he had only done nothing but execute orders. For a moment the doubt entered his mind like a cucaracha slipping under a door.

"No. Do as said" Miranda killed the cucaracha.

"Okay, I'll do it" she confirmed without looking him in the eyes.

"Do you have everything you need?"

"Yup."

The General was impressed that the secret product she had been dragging for days had not yet been found by Rodrìguez's security. Again something was quite wrong.

"The product it's hidden in a place where nobody would find it," she explained, sensing his doubts. Slowly they walked inwards.

Dinner was delicious. Fresh lobsters, pabellon criollo, arepas, empanadas and platanos, all accompanied by an excellent Italian wine.

"How do you find yourself in your new job function?" Rodríguez asked without getting distracted by the food. Miranda noticed that the wedding had done him good. For the first time since he knew him, he seemed relaxed and helpful.

"Very well, Mr. President. Thank you for the opportunity you have given me." He cleaned his lips with the help of the napkin.

"Do you think it will be possible to expand production and increase explorations?" The President asked leaving Miranda stunned.

"I still don't know, but I guess so" he hesitated "Excuse me, Mr. President. There is something I don't quite understand. Perhaps, you can help me," he added taking advantage of the state of grace in which Rodríguez seemed to find himself that evening.

"Sure. Tell me"

"I didn't understand why years ago was taken the decision to reduce production? And again, who made this decision?"

Fernando took a sip of his wine before wiping his mustache and answering. It was a good question, but did Miranda really not know who, and why, had made this decision? Was he so stupid?

"Look," he began, "I will explain the situation in a very simple way, so that my wife also understands. Our country is the largest oil producer in all of South America, which is why others are very interested in us. Now tell me General, how much have foreign powers influenced our internal affairs?"

"Very, very much"

"Exactly! That is the point. Venezuela is like a beautiful woman that everyone wants to take advantage of. And when she withdraws is when, as I say, they give *her the kiss of death*. They destroy it economically, to impoverish it. It's the same strategy that it is adopted with many other countries. Countries that have, like us, resources that others don't have, and that they want to acquire. Or, even worse some countries have the same resources as we do, but they want to keep it aside for when the prices are exorbitant. Now you will be certainly wondering: who really pulls the strings of our economic policies? Unfortunately, it is an answer that I cannot provide. But I invite you to reflect on it, and you will understand for yourself that, deep down in this world, we are all at the mercy of the international economy. One only has to look further to understand it. Believe me: oil is our greatest wealth and our dead sentence, General"

Miranda thought about it. It was not the answer he'd expected. He had always seen Rodríguez making Bolivarian propaganda and today, for the first time, everything he had said was not propaganda at all. Indeed, he had been very specific and realistic. It almost seemed that all his television campaigns, or the river speeches to the nation, were nothing more than a facade, behind which he hid much more. Suddenly, he felt manipulated. What if Cecilia was right? What if by eliminating Rodríguez a worse one had arrived? And how much worse? He continued to eat as if nothing had happened. The platanos were exquisite and Cecilia had changed the subject of the conversation. They were now talking about child education and literacy.

Throughout dinner Fernando thought that something was wrong. Miranda had never been considered a genius, and among other things he was also starting to have an age. It seemed strange to him that he dared to ask him this kind of questions, and he began to think that something strange was going on in the Generals' head. He didn't know what it was, but he thought he might have got some clues by inviting him to make a chat with a good cigar and a glass of wine in their hands, before sending him back home. And so he did.

Sitting on the comfortable leather armchairs of the library, the two men smoked Cuban cigars while enjoying a liquor.

"Our strategy is to sell our oil in emerging markets," explained Rodríguez. "They are the only countries where we do not directly clash with the powers of OPEC and super-powers. What do you think about it?" Rodríguez was trying to make him feel uncomfortable.

"Actually I don't know yet, I haven't had time to get an idea," he apologized.

"But you did noticed that production fell, as consequently did the prices"

"Obviously"

"Indeed. Prices have gone down, and because the Bolívar has been devalued so much is no longer worth anything. Have you seen the price of a packet of rice? It is equivalent to two weeks' salary of a public employee. And do you think I'm going to give the Yankees oil?"

"No."

"For this we need to sell oil immediately. We must attract foreign capital from other countries so that the investors can help us pay for explorations and increase production. Once they have invested, they will not let themselves be commanded because they will want to recover their investment plus the benefit. Do you follow me?"

"Yes." Miranda realized at that moment that the President was very intelligent. "Well. Then I think it wouldn't be bad if you'll accompany me on my travels in Africa and the Middle East. There, we can find the investors we need. According to the calculations, we need $ 20 billion to get the whole system up and running. It is an investment that can be recovered in just six years. I would say figures are highly attractive!"

Miranda was surprised to hear what Rodríguez said. It seemed to him as if he had never known him before. "Are you feeling well? Because you look a bit absent," said Fernando.

"Yes, sorry. Is that I have a bit of high blood pressure lately. It is probably age"

"Okay, I told you everything I had to tell you," he dismissed him.

A while after sitting in the car on his way home, Miranda felt dazed. *The CIA had always told me that Rodríguez had stopped the explorations and reduced official sales, because in reality, together with his friends, they had set up a ghost company that was selling oil outside of the official channels, in the so-called offshore. That's what Carter said to me.* He held his head with both hands. It may be that Cecilia was right, but there was no time to find out everything. It was already too late. In addition, he'd been watched closely. It would have been too risky for him to make any move that was not standard. An idea crept into his thoughts. Even if it was crazy, it was the only thing he could do.

CHAPTER 21

Last supper

The Washington restaurant had been closed for the occasion and Truman was sitting in a chair with a plate of *Bolognese spaghetti* in front of him, which looked disgusting in spite of the $22 price. Truman, who the newspapers called *the leader*, was now shitting in his pants.

"So you're telling me you still haven't solved the Venezuelan problem?" The head of the Oil Association started eating his lasagna on the other side of the table. "Now explain to me why do we grant those CIA motherfuckers an unlimited budget, if they can't solve a problem as simple as this!?"

"They will solve it, they just need more time"

"Do you take me for a fool? You told me the same thing six months ago. I have everything ready. I have investors, contracts, and they are all ready to rush to that shitty country and break their asses deep into the jungle, to extract oil. They are all waiting for you to do your job. We are talking about the first oil company in the world that asks you to get rid of that baboon of Rodríguez! And are you telling me that we have to wait longer? I mean, aren't you supposed to be the American President, the most important man in the world? Let me get this straight. There are only two possibilities: either you are fooling me or someone is poking you!"

"That's what I thought too," he sighed

"Then what are you waiting to find this son of a bitch and get someone from the services to have him *suicided*? I warn you: if the plan fails, in November you will go home"

CHAPTER 22

Chacao

Sitting in a café in the elegant Las Mercedes urbanization, Cecilia was waiting for Antonio. They'd been out of touch since she'd got married to Tom, but now that her face was all over the newspapers, it had not been possible to avoid seeing him again.

Antonio had called that morning to gossip. He wanted her to tell him everything, and started to get really excited. He said how incredible that was: his little witch had really figured that one out, and got it all. He wanted to know all the details. In addition, he resented the fact that he had not been invited to the wedding of the year. In that moment Cecilia understood that the boy was too gossipy and too well introduced to let him wandering around free to speculate on her. It was inappropriate, given her delicate situation. Especially if he would start babbling about Tom Forrester. Antonio was the weak link in the chain, and for this reason she had invited him for a coffee face to face in a chic bar of town. She hadn't still figure out how she could neutralise him. For sure she would had made up something, after all she was used to figure it out things by herself, as usual.

"Hi, little witch" he squeezed her, making the escort immediately react.

"Don't worry, it's nothing," Cecilia instructed them to keep calm

"Hi, slim! How much I've missed you!" Circumstance sentence.

"And I missed you too!" He took off his sunglasses and threw them on the coffee table.

"It's incredible! I haven't heard from you in three years and the last thing I know your face is splashed all over the news! He moved his arms to emphasize the concept."

"As I have said. When you come from nothing as I do, you don't just wait around for occasions to be served on a plated tray." She sipped her passion fruit extract. "How are things going for you?"

"As usual. I work like crazy and the Misses drive me mad, as always. At the House of Dreams everything is always the same. Nothing has changed. Same routine! What about you? How are things going in Europe? Aren't you tired of living in those old cities? When did you come back to Caracas?" He machine-gunned her with questions. Too many questions. She had to stop him.

"I need a favor, Antonio," she said seriously.

"I'm sorry, what? Aren't you the First Lady of Venezuela, and you need a favor from me?"

"Yes," she looked down.

"Hey! What are you sad about? What's the matter with you witch?"

"You see ..." she sighed "recently they've found out that I have cancer" she eyes watered.

"What? How is it possible?" His eyes were out of their sockets.

"I don't know... but you see, at the moment nobody knows. I have to find an oncologist who can cure me here in Caracas. Would you help me?"

"Of course my friend! If you recall, the owner of the Dream House had cancer and one of the best known doctors in Venezuela cured him"

"Call him right away, please." Antonio pulled out his cell

phone immediately and managed to get an appointment for her on that same day. They chatted at the bar for another hour taliking about everything as they used to do back in the old days. Antonio's gossip cravings disappeared just like that.

At three in the afternoon, the car stopped in front of the clinic, in the elegant urbanization of Chacao. Cecilia made the sign of the cross as she waited for the security to open the rear door for her. The Director of the clinic went out to receive her. He was excited because, for the first time ever the First Lady was visiting his clinic, and wanted to prove he was a professional. He noticed the yellow dress that Cecilia wore. She was a woman of spectacular beauty, even more live than in the pictures.

"First Lady! It is a pleasure and an honor to receive you here today!" He showed his white teeth.

"Thanks"

They entered together, walking slowly. As Cecilia instructed the escort to remain outside, they both entered the Director's office, decorated with dozens of awards. Cecilia sat comfortably on the sofa. She intentionally crossed her legs revealing the lace of her stockings she was wearing and noticed that the maneuver had the desired she intended it to have when the Director, began to feel visibly uncomfortable.

"Tell me, what can I do for you?"

"I need something very special from you. In return, I will be very generous." She began to undo the buttons on her dress and then she got up, letting the dress fall to the ground.

CHAPTER 23

Smoke and mirrors

Mulligan waited on the other end of the line for Miranda to go down to the parking lot to be able to speak freely.

"Are you still there?" He checked pulling his cell phone out of his pocket.

"Yes. I want immediate confirmation that everything is proceeding according to plan"

"I saw Cecilia last night. Don't worry, everything will go as planned." Mulligan relaxed for a moment. The General's voice did not reveal any doubts.

"I spoke to her yesterday" he insisted "nothing has changed".

"I hope."

"Believe me. There is nothing to fear. Now that she's with him all day, it's even easier for her to act"

"There is not much time left. Tic Tock...."

"She will act fast, don't worry." Mulligan ended the conversation. If there was a thing he had learned during his career, was that when someone told him not to worry it was time to worry.

He called Agent Maxwell.

"I'm Mulligan"

"Yes sir" she crashed her cigarette on the sidewalk.

"I want you to keep an eye on Miranda. This time we can't go wrong"

"Copied". Maxwell pressed the red button on her phone

to close the conversation and thought Mulligan must had been in deep shit if he called her directly.

Cecilia return to La Casona around 4:30 in the afternoon. As usual, her husband was busy with one of his endless meetings. She went up to their room. Her bodyguards followed her and sat in the corridor just outside her door. She went to the bathroom. It hadn't been pleasant to blow that guy off. But she had managed to get what she wanted, as always she had figured it out. She opened one of her make-up bags and looked for the Estée Lauder's compact powder box. She opened it gently and scrupulously to prevent the transparent plastic that covered it from moving. The first time the CIA had shown her the lethal product, she thought they were joking. But when she saw the effect that this powder had caused on laboratory mices in such a short time, she'd been frightened.

"We bought a normal compact powder, one that is sold everywhere, and replaced the powder with the C39. The jewel of our workshops. The genius idea is that you can take it anywhere with you. It is odorless, colorless, and goes unnoticed. Its effect is triggered only when it comes into contact with water. Nobody will suspect anything. You will carry it in your purse, as if it was an ordinary face powder. But be careful not to breathe it, you never know."

They had explained that, at any moment in which he would be distracted she would had melt it in the President's glass and, a few days later, the symptoms of liver cancer would begin to appear. It would had been a very aggressive and rare cancer. A tumor designed in the CIA laboratory, to get rid of the rough ones, without leaving a trace. A plan worthy the best CIA brains. She put the powder back into her beauty bag and went to the next room where she took out from her purse the fake diagnoses the Director of the clinic had prepared as she had convinced him through her oral performance. She quietly analyzed the first diagnosis to check that the information written down was correct.

Patient: Fernando Rodríguez

Years: 44. She glanced through the medical report looking for the points that she had specifically asked him to write.

Diagnosis: early stage liver cancer.

Second report. Diagnosis: advanced stage liver cancer.

Third report: incurable stage liver cancer.

The dates were spread over several weeks, as she was told by the CIA, the disease would develop. She prayed to Santa Ávila.

"Are you here my love?"

Fernando entered the room adjacent to the bathroom through the door. Cecilia hid everything quickly at the bottom of the drawer where she stored her beauty products.

"I'm here darling!"

"Are you doing your make up? You are already beautiful, why do you need makeup?" He patted her butt affectionately. "Are you OK? They told me you went to the Chacao clinic."

"Yes. I thought that now that I am the First Lady, I will have to help those who suffer, right? So, every day I visit a city hospital to talk to the Directors and see what I can do to help them," she explained.

Fernando thought for a moment that his wife was hiding something from him. But actually, Cecilia was a girl who was used to work. She did not seem the kind of woman who would spend her days at home in laziness. In addition, Fernando, who had been a bachelor for many years now, had forgotten that the First Lady was a relevant figure in the country, especially if her name was Cecilia Mendoza and was a former beauty queen. So he said nothing.

"All right. It seems like a good idea to me." He kissed her

on the lips. "Today your photo is out on all the newspapers in the country," he continued as she looked at him vainly. "You make me proud, you know that? although I should be angry that you are taking the spotlight out of me," he protested.

"That's why you married me. To have a competitor" she joked, knowing that, basically, what she said was true.

"Actually, I hope to have you just for me," he held her in his arms.

"And I'm here for you."

CHAPTER 24

Dobermann

Agent Maxwell followed Miranda and saw that he looked tense. *Where the fuck is he going in the middle of the night?* She snorted seeing that it was 11 pm. Maybe he had a lover, but it seemed strange that he was going to see her now; just when the mission was in its most delicate phase. He stopped the car at a safe distance, far from the General's. The urbanization La Florida was fairly quiet, despite being Caracas one of the most dangerous cities in the world, especially at night. After checking the surrounding to make sure no-one had followed him, Miranda went to the entrance of a house and rang the bell. A Dobermann wandering around the garden barked. The door of the house opened and a woman stepped out. She also checked the surroundings making sure there was no one else but the General. Once reassured she grabbed the dog and let the General in.

Miranda apologized for the slight delay, while the lady led him into the lounge.

"Don't worry, you are here now. Excuse me for calling you in such a rush, but I thought some information might be interesting to you."

"Are we alone?" He made sure, while sitting on the pink sofa and took his hat off.

"Yeah. Sure"

"Do you mind if I take off my jacket? It's very hot"

"Please go ahead" she disappeared into the kitchen and

returned with two glasses of fresh lemonade. He left one of the glasses right in front of him.

"Thanks" he took a long sip. "So tell me"

"Well. I don't know the whole story, but what my husband told me before he was jailed is that the Americans had decided to invest in the Venezuelan oil market."

"When?"

"This was about five years ago. At first my husband thought it was a good thing, but one day he came home very nervous. He said it was a trap and that in this way the Americans would take control over all the benefit, and leave Venezuela empty hand without money and without oil"

"What happened after that?"

"My husband went to talk to President Oriondo about this issue. But then, it doesn't seem to me that Oriondo did anything about it"

"What do you mean?" He said holding the glass in mid-air.

"Apparently, the deal had to be made. So it was decided by the Americans."

"Ma'am, why is your husband in jail, exactly?"

"My husband was against signing the agreement under those conditions, but Oriondo eventually forced him to sign it. To convince him, he gave him a huge sum of money. So in the end my husband Lucas signed. But things were not going well. They raid on our only source of income. They forced us to sell them our oil below the market price. When Rodríguez arrived he immediately realized the situation. He called my husband to get an explanation about what was happening and my husband explained it to him. The President was furious. It was on that day that he froze our bank accounts and had my poor husband put in prison, charged of collaborating in favor of foreign companies to the detriment of the nation. The head of the Oil Association was hysterical! He even called me!"

"The Oil Association?"

"Yup. That is how it is called: Oil Association. My husband hated them! Now, they've got this gentleman to be President. They think they can replicate what they had done with Oriondo, but as they say, turned out to be a fiasco!"

"Excuse me, I don't understand. Are you referring to the new President of the Oil Association? "

"Of course not! I am talking about the new President of Venezuela: Rodríguez!" Miranda went white as a rag.

"Are you ok? You don't look so well, you know? Do you want a Colombian coffee? My friend from Bogota brings me a pack every time she comes to Caracas."

"Are you telling me that Rodríguez became President with the American support?" His eyes where were wide open in surprise.

The lady gave him a sceptical look "Of course, General! You're funny. Where did you live till now on the moon? Of course it is like that! It has always been like that! The Americans first help them to get in the position, and then, when things get out of their hands, they want to get rid of them. You must not have been around here much during your career." She taunted him. She was right Miranda had spent his career in the south of the country, very far from the Federal District.

He started analysing the facts from another point of view. What if they had told him a myriad of nonsense for him to believe. So that he would not rise any doubt. They'd showed him what they wanted him to see: a country in disarray, an authoritarian President, a system of poverty due to the President's madness, and corruption. What system isn't corrupted anyway?

"What I would like to say is that my husband is innocent. The President was wrong. My Lucas has always been against American interferences in our internal affairs. It was

Oriondo who sold the country to the Yankees. What could my poor husband do?"

Maxwell answered immediately on the first ring.

"Tell me Mulligan, what did you find?"

"It's the house of the wife of the former Director of the Venezuelan national oil company. You have to take them down". He ordered

"Both?"

"Yes"

Maxwell racked her gun to check how many bullets she had left in the barrel. It was full. She got out of the car silently and walked down on her knees towards the wall of the house which was so low that it was difficult for her to hide behind it. One foot after another, she approached the entrance. The nostrils of the Dobermann that was unleashed in the garden began to move, perceiving her smell in the air. An intense trail of adrenaline the animal immediately recognized. It was getting closer. His primordial instinct did not betray him, as he snapped following that scent with his sharp teeth on display. He started to growl. Hearing the dog growl Miranda immediately understood what was going on. Someone had come to kill them and he was not appointed by Rodríguez. He pushed the lady to the ground and threw himself next to her. She baffled and got frightened for a moment not understanding what the General was doing. He worryingly glanced at her.

"Don't move. Someone is here to kill us."

He saw the lady's eyes turn into glass. It was the effect of fear. Fear. That emotion that, during military training, they teach you not to feel. But now, Miranda was afraid. He pulled out his gun. Although he had never been considered a genius, he knew that going to see his predecessor's wife was among the riskiest moves he could do.

Maxwell gently opened the wrought iron gate to avoid making any noise. In total silence, the dog's dark eyes followed her every move in preparation for the attack. The agent slipped the gun cannon between the iron bars. Seeing the reflection of the metal in the darkness, the animal jumped forward, and with the impetus and precision that nature had given him, he attacked like a ferocious killer. Maxwell watched him soaring upwards with his teeth unsheathed and pride in his eyes. She waited for him to get into the firing line and, when he did she pulled the trigger just once. The animal fell instantly to the ground as if its body had been struck by a lightning. A single bullet, right in the center of those eyes designed to terrify, and which now looked at her lifeless. The victory of human intelligence over animal power. With the gun in both hands, she approached the window. The house seemed empty. Miranda had figured out what was about to happen, so she had to proceed very carefully now. Crawling on the stone ground, Miranda and the lady approached the kitchen door. From there they could have gone out into the garden, and run away by car. The precision of that maneuver would have saved their lives or not. He had to prove he was better than a CIA agent. Not that it was easy given his age. But now both their lives were in his hands. He rubbed against the wall. Not knowing where Maxwell could be hiding, he had to be careful not to get on the line of fire. Being in a single-story house he knew they were easy targets. The agent could easily have shot him from any window. In the apparent quiet of the house, the General closed his eyes, thus amplifying the perception of sounds.

It was a tactic he had used frequently when he fought in the forest; inside that thick vegetation that did not allow you to see not even the sky. Now, with his eyes closed, he clearly felt the beat of his pulse. He was totally focused.

With precision worthy of his training, Maxwell, who

was stationed outside the window, aimed at the edge of the wall. Sooner or later they would move, and she would have killed them both exactly as she had liquidated the dog. Miranda knew she would never enter the house. In fact, she had walled them inside. Getting carried away by instinct, Miranda bet that Maxwell was outside the kitchen window. Stuck between the edge of the cabinet and the dining table, he knew that she would tirelessly stay out there for hours if it were necessary, waiting for them to move. He therefore decided to put into practice a deterrent tactic. With two fingers of his right hand he took the edge of the tablecloth of the kitchen table and pulled hard. The dishes on the table fell to the ground breaking into a thousand pieces; that would have distracted Maxwell. Maxwell fired several times near the edge of the cabinet. Miranda had been smart in hiding inside the kitchen cabinet, whose top was made of unbreakable marble. Now he knew exactly where she was, when he retrieved the tablecloth in his hands, he threw it into the air, firing a rapid sequence of bullets, towards the point where Maxwell was. He wounded her in the arm. This gave him a maximum of five seconds to escape. With force and decision, he tugged the lady by her arm.

"Where is your car?" Miranda knew that the first thing Maxwell had done was to cut his car's tires.

"In the garage," hissed the woman.

"Then run!"

They both ran to the garage. The old lady's Toyota Corolla was fortunately parked inside the garage, so Maxwell had not been able to tamper with it. Not that it was the most suitable type of car for the circumstances, but he'll make it work. The lady grabbed the handle of the car and held her breath. What her husband had told her was, in fact, a sweetened version of reality.

"Hold on!" Cried the General starting off in a rocket. A

volley of bullets riddled the car door with absolute precision. Trying not to lose control of the vehicle, Miranda fired a few shots, but without hitting Maxwell.

The agent's arm ached as Maxwell was losing a lot of blood but she couldn't let them get away. Now, the entire Orinoco Operation was at risk of being revealed and she had to take them out of the picture before Miranda could tell everything. Maxwell got in the car and accelerated. She could still see the Toyota Corolla at the bottom of the slope.

CHAPTER 25

Miranda

Cecilia tried to get in touch with Miranda. His cell phone was always turned off. She thought it was a little strange, but not so much. People the General's age usually had no symbiotic relationship with their phones. She looked at the large clock on the library table. It was almost midnight. She allowed herself a few minutes of relaxation, throwing an eye on the photos circulating about her on social networks and on Google. Her image was everywhere. In the meantime, her husband was, as usual, busy talking to someone in the office in the next room. With a little effort, Cecilia could have listened to the conversation, but in the end she didn't care much. She had taken her decision, and so she could start to relax a little. *I'll give Miranda the fake reports, so they think I poisoned him which I didn't.* In that precise moment the word Orinoco surfaced in the conversation between her husband and the guy with whom he was talking. She looked up from his smartphone screen and pricked up her ears.

Have they discovered the Orinoco Operation! Fuck!

The person who was talking to her husband, said that the CIA had resumed funding for the Orinoco Operation, and that a new attack would therefore have to be expected. The President let him speak without interrupting.

I know the President thought.

Cecilia understood that this was to be the mole. Mulligan had in fact mentioned that the previous operations had always disastrously failed because of a still unidentified spy. She tried to associate that voice to a face. Who was he? She couldn't tell. Anyway it didn't matter as her days were numbered. As soon as someone had mentioned her name involved into the Orinoco Operation she would had little time left to live. She would have died young at the age of 27. It wouldn't have helped trying to convince Fernando that she had only been used. That they had left her with no choice and that in the end, she had also fallen in love with him. Which was true. A man like Fernando would not have believed her. And even if he believed her, he wouldn't have forgiven her.

CHAPTER 26

The Hour of Truth.

Across the city, the Toyota Corolla was launched at full speed on the sloping streets of La Florida urbanization. In the dark of the night, with very few street lamps working, Miranda chose not to turn on the headlights, to confuse Maxwell who was glued behind his car. Not even with the most reckless maneuvers had he managed to get her out of his way.

Shit!! He went down the slopes of La Florida as a rocket, desperately trying to get to the Los Caobos Urbanization. He could not risk taking the highway. That piece of junk he was driving would not speed up to 160 km per hour while downhill, and Maxwell would have reached them in a snap. He then decided to slip through the narrow streets of Santa Rosa, and then proceed to Santo Augustin del Norte; arriving at Vista Alegre from where, he would have entered the road of La Guaira, and then proceed westwards until arriving at La Casona. There was no other place to go. He would explain to the President the trap he'd fell into and tell him the whole truth. He would die in every way, but at least with honor. As it should have been for a brave General who sacrificed himself for his homeland and his people, as he'd always did. Zigzagging he proceeded through the narrow streets he had known since his childhood. The car skidded when cornering due to the high speed. He was driving aggressively, honking to everyone who approached his trajectory. He did not stop on red traffic lights.

However, he tried to drive so that Maxwell could not overtake him. He remembered those very risky manoeuvres, which he had carried out several times in other similar situations, in which he had found himself during his career. Just when the agent's black car was about to pass him, he pulled the handbrake. His heart stopped beating for an instant, while the car started spinning abruptly on itself. The lady next to him propped herself up against everything she could find and started screaming. In that whirlpool, the General noticed that the car was dangerously approaching the edge of the fountain. It was at that moment that he shifted gear and pressed on the accelerator. The Toyota jumped before responding to commands. Now, he found himself in the wrong direction on the square, and the General cut to take the road he wanted to take. Maxwell, increasingly weakened by the wound, could not keep up with him.

Hidden behind her husband's office door, Cecilia had heard everything. Fernando was as calm as always. The thing was surprising. Or not? One thing was certain: you never knew what Fernando was thinking. Fortunately, her name -Cecilia- had never been mentioned in the conversation between the two, but how long would it take Fernando before putting the pieces of the puzzle together? As soon as the man took his leave, Cecilia quickly hid in the adjoining lounge. She threw herself into an armchair, as if she had been laying there for hours; lost in her thoughts of Miss. She waited to see if, once alone, the features of her husband's face would reveal some emotion. Nothing. His expression, which she peeped through the glass, did not seem to be changing.

She therefore discarded the idea that he knew the truth about her. After all, how could he suspect her? She had been very cautious, and had played her role perfectly. So good that he fell in love with her and brought her to the altar. She saw him run a hand over his mustache. Usually he did this when he was thinking. *Now he's probably thinking about how to get rid of me. He will have me killed and make sure my body is never to be found again.* She knew that sooner or later that would had been her destiny waiting to happen. A shiver ran down her spine.

"Cecilia !?" Rodríguez appeared in the doorway by taking off his jacket and propping it on a finger behind his shoulder. He found his wife sitting in the large lounge chair. Without shoes, she had a leg dangling from the armrest. Her eyes were fixed on her smartphone.

"What's so interesting?" He approached. Cecilia stretched her arms pretending to yawn, as if she was a bit rattled and ready for bed. Rodríguez smiled and sat down on the pouf next to her.

"What are you doing here honey?" He said with the characteristic smiling tone he used with her. "Nothing my love. I was falling asleep while looking at my Instagram"

"How many followers do you have?" He asked

"Half of Venezuela" she scratched her nose. Her husband looked at her gently. "Are you done with your meeting?" she faked total disinterest in his reply.

"Yup." He said dryly

"Was it interesting?" Her heart began to rush.

"Not so much." He said sibylline. Cecilia expected him to tell her about the Orinoco Operation that her informant had discovered. And instead he said a simple "Shall we go to bed?"

He held out his hand to help her up. She got up, and as she was bare feet left her long, rainbow-colored chiffon dress rub against the black and white marble floor. At that moment, the scream of the sirens interrupted the relaxed atmosphere in which only crickets were heard singing in the garden.

"President!" Screamed out loud the security chief who bursted into the salons "There is an emergency!" He looked very worried.

"What happened?" Fernando said in a colorless tone of voice.

"Mister President! Excuse the intrusion but it is very urgent! It's General Miranda! He's here! He says he has to talk to you about something very important and urgent. A red code! Among other things, he arrived in a completely wrecked car accompanied by a lady in her seventies. He says she is the wife of the former Director of the Venezuelan oil company," he exclaimed.

"Get him," Fernando ordered, a little annoyed by all this hustle and bustle that arose just when he was about to go to sleep.

"Right away, sir. They say they were attacked, apparently." The head of security seemed very eager.

"OK it's good. I get it. Get them through!" Fernando imagined that it was going to be a long night and this did him no pleasure.

Meanwhile, in Cecilia's head the words were bundled with the echo. The showdown had come. The hour of truth. She bit her tongue from the stress. Her nostrils dilated and she began to breathe deeply. *Now, they'll bring out the whole truth and then kill me! I don't want to die! I'm only 27! It's not fair! I didn't want to get involved into all this mess. It should be Mulligan who gets the consequences of this!*

In that instant Miranda entered the main door, accompanied by a lady in her seventies. A short and thin woman, dressed in a pink dress down to her knees. Her skin was so thin that her veins could be seen in transparency. In her eyes you could read everything that she had been through that day.

She seemed quite shocked. Even the General was wrinkled with a short-sleeved shirt that partially sticked out of his pants. It was supposed that he had left home in a suit and tie, but there was no trace of his jacket. He had left it in the La Floresta villa. Both of them had disheveled hair and in their faces, pale as those of someone who has seen a ghost, one could see the typical symptoms of post traumatic shock, which Rodríguez recognized immediately.

"What happened?" Rodríguez analyzed the state in which they were.

"President ... we have been attacked..." the voice was struggling to get out of the vocal cords as it was exhausted. "Mr. President ... the Americans ..." he leaned on the entrance console.

"Sit down, please," Cecilia invited them, showing to them two comfortable sofas.

"Bring some water!" She ordered to an assistant who was standing to the side, not knowing what to do. She then took a pashmina and placed it over her own shoulders as she was starting to feel cold.

"It's just that I don't know where to start ..." the General was almost about to cry.

"Mr. President" began the lady "they tried to kill us tonight because I told General Miranda all the intrigues that your predecessor, President Oriondo had hatched with the American Government".

"Mmm," Rodríguez muttered, not at all impressed. "Go on, please," he urged.

"You are right, Mr. President. The Yankees have armed a conspiracy against you." Miranda emptied a whole glass of water. When he finished, Cecilia filled it up again for him.

Rodríguez looked at all the three in their eyes. He closed his fist and placed his knuckles on his hip. A movement he often made when he wanted to put others in difficulty.

"I already know this. And I also know that you are a CIA spy." He let the phrase echoed in everyone's heads.

Miranda could not believe to his ears. "You knew?" He instinctively covered his face with both hands in shame.

"Yes General. I know." His black eyes blazed. He looked at Miranda's face for a long minute in disarray. Those little eyes come out of their sockets. How much it amused him to make people uncomfortable, and the feeling of power he got from it. He had them all there trapped like rats.

"But if you knew ... why ... why didn't you say anything-" he stammered

"-You are wrong General," he interrupted. Then he paused, getting up from the sofa. He went to the window and looked out towards the La Casona gardens.

Cecilia thought that they had all failed. Her, the CIA, Miranda and everyone else involved in this operation. Suddenly, she realized that the operation had failed and that her deal with CIA would blow up in smoke. She could say *Sayonara* to her 20 million dollars that vanished before her eyes. *Shit!* Once again she would had gone back from where she'd started, without money, without a husband, without anything! But then she thought that it was no longer important for she would never come out of here alive.

The President poured himself a drink. "You see General. There is a basic rule in war. Keep your friends close and your enemies closer. I didn't say it. Sun Tzu said it in his book 'The Art of War'." He explained before the General's glazed eyes. "I'm surprised that you don't know this quote, General," he said with a look of superiority. Miranda no longer knew where to hide his disgrace, while Cecilia tried to think about the consequences of all this. Miranda had studied Sun Tzu, but he didn't expect to fall into such a refined and Machiavellian trap, set by someone like Rodríguez, who hadn't even attended school. This man had a superior mind. What his family nonexistent economic means had not offered him, God had given him in intelligence. For a moment he would have liked to understand how he thought. Entering his so perfect brain to find out how it worked, and how sophisticated it was.

"But I still don't understand why ..." Miranda said finally.

"Dear General," he teased him a little. "I'm sorry to hear that you think I'm a perfect idiot. What do you think, that I didn't know the CIA would visit you? Do you really think I don't know how the system works? There is a reason if you are a General ... and I am the President." He prayed and Miranda gave it to him. "I know everything, because I can read behind people's faces. You are a *pasionario* of your country, you were born like that and you'll die like that. You have no own ideas you just get influenced by ideals. Country. Honor. Respect." he emphatically said.

"This all sounds very good, doesn't it? But as you see, the world doesn't work like that. These ideals, however noble, always lead to catastrophe. In fact, they led you towards the abyss. Accept me advice: you have to be pragmatic in this life, General." The escort gasped over hearing the President speak. This was the President they liked. Calm, serious, intelligent, strong-willed.

"Where is my phone," he asked to his assistant. Fernando inhaled deeply and intoned some notes of a song which, as usual, he did not remember the words.

"Here it is!"

"Look for yourself." He showed his phone's contacts list scrolling down to letter C." Look carefully. What's written there?"

Miranda's eyes grew large with surprise. "But this is ... it is ... the ..." He couldn't pronounce it. Rodríguez decided to help him. "Yes, General. Exactly it. It's Carter's number! The head of the CIA, the man who has played you this whole time like a puppeteer since you'd met him"

The President couldn't make himself clearer.

As for Cecilia, she could not believe it. How was that possible? And why all these intrigues?

The President sat back on the sofa sipping his drink, to which he had added a pinch of angostura.

"You didn't expect that, did you? As you see, the Americans kicked your ass too"

"Since when did you know?" Miranda asked

"What, that you collaborate with them? Since always. That's why I put you in charge of the oil company. It was the perfect excuse to make you see with your own eyes the intrigues and the felonies that happen behind those ideals for which you sacrificed your whole life. And I'd like to point out that in this world nothing is black and white. Everything is grey."

"And now, will you kill me?" Miranda's eyes got filled with despair. Not only had he served his country faithfully, thinking he was doing good, but he had been duped twice.

"Kill you? As a national hero? God no! No way! And why? So then after can arrive other stupid idiots like you, or worse than you? The defenders of loyalty? Another prick that the CIA can manipulate, in order to kill me? Nah!" He made a strange grimace with his face. "The truth is, I believe in redemption, and in the fact that you have learned your lesson. You know how they say: a Christian converted from another religion is better than an atheist." Miranda thought he was right.

"You will continue to take charge of the oil company. We have hot billionaire deals soon to be signed with other countries. So get ready-"

"-What do I tell to Mulligan?" He jumped up worried.

"Ah! Ah! General! this is your problem! I don't care." He gave him what he deserved.

"But the CIA will kill me!" He fidgeted. Rodríguez's eyes

looked at him as if he were talking about time, not death.

"Probably yes. In fact, I would almost certainly say, now that I think about it that your days are counted, but not my problem." He Exclaimed. He loved playing with people's emotions. "But don't you think I've been magnanimous enough to spare your life, General?" Miranda had no choice but to nod.

"Well, then as you certainly will understand I will leave your problems in your hands" He stated. *That son of a bitch!* Not only had he manipulated it as he wanted, but now he'd left Miranda carrying the problem in his hands. The President emptied his glass of rum in one breath, and got up from the sofa. He offered his hand to his wife.

"By the way. I will pass you some documents on the national oil company. They are for your eyes only very strictly confidential sort of documents, which are currently hidden in the island of Aruba. There you'll will find all the explanations to your questions. In addition to all the illegal traffics that have been made from 1980 to today, between the Venezuelan oil company and the Oil Association now if you would excuse me...". He walked towards the staircase. The seventy-year-old lady, who until now had kept quiet and silent on the sidelines, but had carefully followed everything the President had said, suddenly said "Mr. Rodríguez. It may be that you are not a great President. But you are an incredibly intelligent and prepared man."

"Give me a few more years, madame and you will see the results with your own eyes. Anyway, don't worry, your husband is fine" he consoled her.

"Yes? Is my Lucas okay?" she brought one hand to her chest excited, while with the other she clenched Rodríguez's hand in hers.

"You will see him very soon. Don't worry, I'll take care of him," he added.

The next day he would free him and send them together to spend the little time they had left to live on an island in the Caribbean. It was the right thing to do.

The security chief reappeared in the doorway out of the blue.

"Mister President! We took Maxwell. What do we do with her?" The President smiled to himself.

"For the moment nothing. Put her in the security room and leave her there, under close surveillance, until further notice!"

"Yes Sir," he went to attention and disappeared.

Maxwell and Mulligan will not suspect anything about my secret relationship with Carter and our fantastic plan, Rodríguez thought. "Well, ladies and gentlemen. I think it's time to go to bed. It's actually two in the morning. Come on, Cecilia!" He began to climb the stairs, squeezing his wife's hand into his.

As Cecilia walled up behind him silently she pulled up the edge of the beautiful colored dress she was wearing.

"Miranda!" Rodrìguez stopped suddenly and turned glancing at him. "Don't even think about going back to your house. Sleep here in the guesthouse. It will be safer."

"Thank you Mr. President." That night Miranda thought that Rodríguez was, after all, a good man.

Cecilia had a heavy heart. As he went up those stairs, as if going to the gallows, her feet where heavy as stones. Now, that she would be alone with him, would he slap her? She knew how violent men in her country could be. And she was afraid Fernando would beat her. Unexpectedly, Rodríguez acted as if nothing had happened. He went to the bathroom, brushed his teeth, put on his pajamas, and slipped under the bed covers. Just as if nothing had ever happened. Cecilia was dismayed.

"Don't you ask me anything?" she peered at him while sitting on the edge of the bed.

"No. What should I ask you?" He stared at the ceiling.

"I don't know, but wow! Does everything that happened tonight seems normal to you?" Her eyes were out of her sockets.

Ah! Women. Why do they always want to talk, for God sakes! He thought. He turned to her and propped up his elbow on the pillow.

"Come on! Spill it. What do you want me to ask you?"

"Are you kidding me?" She unleashed her South American temper.

"No! It's that I don't understand you. We have been talking about this topic for over an hour downstairs. What do you want me to ask you? To a Miss?" He planted his gaze inside her eyes. She confronted that gaze as her brain processed the puzzle pieces in order logically. Or at least, she tried to.

"What if ..." she started to say but he silenced her with a kiss

"Go to sleep, it's already two in the morning," he turned on the other side and closed his eyes

"No! I want to talk to you! I want you to know!" she still wanted to chat. Fernando snorted, turning to face her once more.

"Cecilia. Whatever it is you want to tell me, I don't want to know it, seriously darling get some sleep." He kissed her good night on the lips and turned for the umpteenth time, this time with his back towards her.

"But do you know that I was ordered to kill you?" Cecilia just couldn't keep the information to herself.

"You? Ahahahaha! You for sure have a wild creativity, my love!" this time he didn't even turn around.

Did he really not know?! This man was worse than a puzzle!

"Fernando. I swear. I had to kill you" she was confessing, and he didn't believe her!

"Okay. But you didn't kill me so, now sleep" was his reply just to make her happy.

"And what do you know? Maybe I did!" she challenged him. Fernando had a lot of fun when she thought she was smarter than he was.

"Shhhhhh!!" He shut her up. "All right, secret agent. Go to sleep!" He turned off the light and went to sleep with his back towards her.

CHAPTER 27

Scarlet Macaws

The next day Rodríguez woke up early. Cecilia was sleeping next to him. Her beautiful chestnut-colored hair, scattered across the pillow, shone illuminated by the beams of light that filtered through the window. He tried not to wake her. He went to the bathroom and then to the walk-in closet, where he put on the light linen suit for the day. He went down to the dining room. A quiet day finally, although he still had to decide what to do with Maxwell and Miranda. As soon as he sat down at the table, he rubbed his eyes. A few steps away from him, just outside the big door window, a couple of scarlet macaws had reached to the ground in search of food. He threw some pieces of bread in their direction and remembered his childhood. When, like all children in his village, he played with wild macaws and used to give them seeds. *Someday I'll fly away from here just like you do* he would think to himself when the birds would fly away into the blue sky. His grandmother, who looked after him and his 3 brothers when their father was looking for work and their mother was selling necklaces at the market, had told them that they were lucky. Because they lived in the most beautiful country in the world, and that when God created it, he had made it the same as paradise. In this way, he and his brothers, even if they had no money nor shoes, had always thought that Venezuela was paradise. The images of that simple life that he had lived as a child, now flowed like a film in his head, giving him a strong nostalgia.

Her grandmother hadn't had time to see what that little boy who loved to play in mud, had become. They hadn't found the money to cure her. $ 50. What was 50 dollars for an American? Nothing. For them it meant losing a loved one. That was why, as soon as he became President, he had strengthened the welfare state.

He took a sip of the watermelon juice, in front of him and asked his assistant to handle him over his mobile phone. He scrolled through the numbers in the directory and called Carter on his private line. "Hi! How are you? How are things going?" Chuckles

"Hi Fernando. I am fine, and you?" He was dressing up to go to work.

"Well. It has been quite a night around here."

Carter couldn't refrain from laughing "I know! I would have paid to be there."

"You can't even imagine." Fernando cupped his chin on his hand.

"And what does Miranda say?" He switched on the hand free to wear his tie.

"I put him in a place where he can refresh his ideas..."

"Really"

"He was shitting his pants" he explained

"I can imagine. Tell me, what do we do with the old woman's husband?" Carter said.

"I will release him out of jail. Then it's up to you. If you want, I can send him to you, well wrapped up with a nice bow around his neck he joked. "If not, I will send them both off to a Caribbean island where they can enjoy the little time they have left to live. But in short, it's your decision!"

Carter laughed. "Honestly the story of the bow intrigues me. It would be a good surprise to have him sent over to the boss of the Oil Association. Who knows. Maybe he would be happy to give him a job. Ah, by the way, you should see Truman's face"

"God, don't mention him to me, please. After all we have done to get rid of him"

"I know. You had your revenge. Truman is cursing you. At least now we are one hundred percent sure that that imbecile will go home in November."

The plan that Carter and Rodríguez had implemented against President Truman and with the support of the Oil Association, had worked perfectly.

"Well. With whom will you replace him in the next elections? " he asked.

"Someone good, don't worry. You will like him"

"I hope. And so? Won't you tell me the name of the next President of the USA?" He sipped his juice.

"No. I'll make you a surprise!" Typical Carter.

"As long as he is not like the thin one with the hoarse voice that was in charge before Truman. That was a total imbecile!"

"Don't worry, you will be happy. By the way. I received your gift." He changed the subject.

"And I have received yours," he said, looking down at his new diamonds encrusted gold Rolex.

"By the way. Tell me something. When will the contract with China be ready?"

"I have it right here, in the safe."

"Good. You know the other day I had lunch with the Director of the Oil Association. He said that the agreement between the Oil Association and the Chinese Oil Company is ready. They have a deal. They already agreed on the percentages so that everyone will take advantage of it, and everyone is happy".

Finally! Fernando thought. After so many struggles the plan had worked. The billions of the investors would flow to Venezuela in a few months. That would bring money, and an economic boost that had never been seen before. The health system would return to function, as well as the school system, tourism, construction and business. At that moment Fernando felt really proud of the enormous work he had carried out.

"Are you still there Fernando?" Carter said given the long silence on the other edge of the phone.

"Yes, I'm here," he brought himself back into the conversation.

"What are you thinking about?"

"That your friends at the Oil Association are rushing"

"Sure! Obviously! We are talking about business worth billions! And control of 80% shares of the oil market in the world."

"As well as the boost of the economy of Venezuela," underlined Fernando.

"Yes, Carter said," exiting the walk-in closet. That particular element was not exactly on the top of his priorities. "By the way. My banker in Panama called me the other day. He wants to know how to arrange things, if you understand what I mean..."

"Tell him not to worry. Everything will be ready for August," he cut short.

"Perfect. So I can buy myself a yacht as big as yours."

"Now don't exaggerate! It must be at least a couple of meters smaller than mine, otherwise I am offended."

Carter laughed. He knew that Rodríguez always wanted to be top of his class. He was like that.

"By the way. You didn't tell me the main thing."

"What??" he pursed his lips. There was nothing more important to him than what they had already talked about.

"What will you do with her?" Carter was really curious.

"You know! It took me 44 years to find her and, with or without your permission, I won't give her back to you"

"Incredible! You liked that girl from the first moment

you laid eyes on her. When she won the beauty contest. Ah! *L'amour!*" He teased him.

"It was just like that," Rodríguez admitted.

"And what about her? Does she want to be with you?"

"I don't know yet, but I'll let her decide."

Carter had the feeling that Cecilia had already decided. But he didn't say it loud. He didn't even mention anything about Tom Forrester, Cecilia's American husband. Who was still locked up in a prison in Nebraska. Now that the deal had been successfully completed, he would have had him released on bail.

"Okay then, keep me up to date, you know I'm a sentimental," he joked. "Now I have to run to the office. Today I have to deal with Iran."

"I don't envy you at all"

"Pfff!" Carter snorted.

Rodríguez ended the call. Everything had gone smoothly, just as it should.

CHAPTER 28

Veneziola

The pirogue glided sharply over the water which was red for its high concentration of minerals.

"Don't lean out of the boat, please. The piranhas jump out of the water in a flash." The head of the security was talking from the bow.

At the rear of the boat, Cecilia was very excited. It was her first time in the middle of the Amazon rainforest and down in the Bolívar State. Canaima National Park was considered to be one of the most beautiful parks in the world. She had read it in the guide. And the Salto Ángel, with its 979 meters high, was the highest waterfall in the world.

She breathed deeply, her lungs filling up with the moisty tropical air the Amazon forest. Fernando, who sat beside her, looked at her ecstatically.

"You didn't bring me here to throw me to the piranhas, didn't you?" She inquired.

Fernando smiled. His wife was unique. Resting with both hands on the edge of the pirogue she looked even younger than her 28 years old.

"I have a surprise for you, honey."

Cecilia rolled her eyes in joke. *Let's see what he had invented this time?*

"Look!" He pointed a finger towards the lush vegetation. On the edge of the *Caroni* river, a huge palafitte sticked out of the dense vegetation. Cecilia instinctively covered her mouth with both hands in surprise.

"Is this yours!?" She was intrigued.

"Well, it's not really mine. *It's ours,*" he smiled.

"Oh, dear! It's spectacular!" she got excited. Once again his chest was filled with pride. He had managed to surprise her again.

"I told you, we live in paradise"

The pirogue approached the private pier of the house. Cecilia got out by grabbing the arm of the boy of the staff who welcomed them.

As soon as she was inside, she wandered around admiring the simple yet beautiful structure which was perfectly inserted into the environment. Even the furniture, which adorned the space, as well as the paintings hanging on the walls, were hand made by the *Yanomamo* tribe.

"Welcome to Venezuela! My love!" Fernando held her in his powerful arms.

"Venezuela or *Veneziola*?" she teased him.

"Venezuela! Without any doubt!" He joked.

Cecilia gave him a look that said it all. She suspected that her husband had built this house only in response to the fact that, months earlier, she had caught it off guard. It was in fact her who had explained the etymology of the word Venezuela to him. For once, he had been bullied and she knew he couldn't get over with it.

Fernando sensed her thought and drowned the giggle that would expose him.

This woman knew him well. So well that she knew his weaknesses and the fact that he had to excel in everything. Besides, she was like that too. The two of them were the same. He kissed her on her bare shoulder.

Cecilia went out the balcony to admire those spectacular square-shaped plateaus the *tepuy*, typical of that region. One in particular was majestic. It was called *Auyantepui*. From the top of it the thin line of water would create the

Salto Ángel. The highest waterfall in the world. Suddenly she realized that no one had ever mentioned Tom again. She thought that maybe one day she should have mentioned Tom to Fernando. Just as a matter of honesty. But then she thought that since he hadn't noticed, she could had avoided it. It would have been her secret. The secret she would take to the grave with her.

Behind him the President was staring at her back. His eyes filled with that beautiful sight. The impenetrable Amazon rainforest, the impressive *tepuy* that stranded tall above the vegetation. The red river that flowed majestically. And that splendid figure in the shadow: Cecilia. Leaning against the balustrade suspended over the river, she smiled happily. For the first time in her life, she felt completely satisfied.

Fernando smiled to himself
Here goes missis Forrester.

He thought. He had finally succeeded in winning Cecilia's heart. And she hadn't even noticed.

END

Index

Printed by Printforce, United Kingdom